HIS FAKE WEDDING DATE

ELLE WATERS

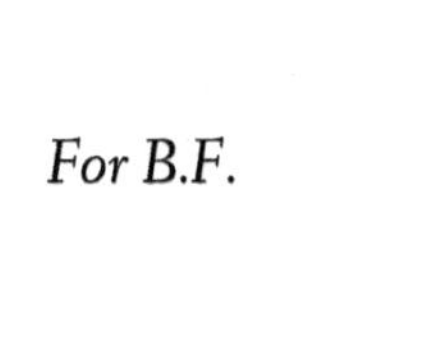

For B.F.

ONE

"SO I TALKED to Mom yesterday and she said she hasn't gotten your response."

Hunter sandwiches the phone between his shoulder and his ear to have both hands free to fumble with the coffee maker. It's way too early to have this conversation without caffeine. Jillian has a habit of calling early in the morning. She's too thoughtful to forget about the three-hour time difference between New York and California, but she knows he's typically an early riser. She's probably been up for hours, already kicking ass and saving lives at the hospital. Hunter, meanwhile, had overslept after staying up too late looking at the specs on a used Cessna he's considering buying, and now he has to hustle to get to work by the morning meeting.

"My response?"

"For the wedding, dummy. I know you got the invite, and I need to know if you're coming. Please say you're coming."

"When is it again?" His attempt at stalling is

completely transparent. He's had the date on his calendar for weeks.

"June twenty-fifth. At Atkins Farm." Jillian sighs. "I need you to be there, Hunter. Please."

Hunter already knows he has to be there. He's about to sigh and make a lightly snarky comment about clearing his schedule, but Jillian's next words surprise him. "And I want you to bring a date."

"A date?"

"You do date, don't you Hunter?" Jillian says, but her tone has turned careful and Hunter's stomach churns. He hates it when she treats him with kid gloves, like something fragile, something breakable.

"Of course I do." He's a thirty-five-year-old single man. He's been on plenty of dates. He just doesn't feel the need to mention they're all first dates. Second date is not in his vocabulary. Never more than a drink, maybe dinner, maybe a hook-up if the other party also isn't interested in anything longer term. The best thing about first dates is there's no history. No baggage. You can pretend to be normal for a night. A second date means the other person might want to learn things about you. And Hunter knows they won't like what they find out. So he saves everyone the trouble.

Unfortunately, you can't take a first date to your ex-wife's wedding.

"Hunter? You there?"

"What? Yeah, just trying to make some coffee."

Jillian laughs and for a second Hunter misses her. Really misses her. She has a lovely, throaty laugh. "So, you're coming and you're bringing someone."

Hunter spills the full filter of coffee grounds on the counter before he can get it in the machine and barely stops himself from swearing. "Yeah. Sure. I'll bring someone."

"What's their name?"

This brings Hunter up short. "Uh. Why do you need to know?"

"For the seating chart, hello."

"Oh right." He sweeps the spilled grounds back into the filter, ignoring the stray crumbs that have been collected along with them.

"Maybe if we hadn't eloped you would know this stuff."

He tries not to take it as a dig. Tries not to picture their wedding, rushed, informal. Jillian wearing scrubs and him in his motorcycle jacket and boots. Candy bars from the vending machine instead of cake.

"So, name?"

Hunter knows he can put her off. But the wedding is in two weeks and he figures her mom really does need to know. He's always liked Myrna, hates the idea of making her life harder because of his bullshit. *Wedding date.* *Wedding date.* His gaze catches on the SkyTrip company calendar. The picture for June is his favorite—the entire team, all six of them, wearing SkyTrip T-shirts and posing in front of their signature blue-on-white airplane. Will, Louis, Isabelle, Laney, all lined up in the back, and in the front, Hunter and Devin, kneeling side by side.

"Devin."

"Devin?" Jillian's voice has something in it that Hunter can't quite read.

"Yeah, Devin. Well, you can tell your mom Devin. Smith. He's my date."

"Wait, Devin? From your work?"

"Problem?" He's a little surprised she places the name so quickly. But Devin's been with him since the beginning of SkyTrip. Three years now. Long enough for Jillian to have heard the name.

"No. It's fine." But there's still something in her voice.

"Fine. great. Listen, Jill, I gotta run."

"See you soon, Hunter."

Hunter clicks the phone off and stabs a button on the coffee maker. It makes a sad gurgling sound, sparks fly, and the light goes out.

Fuck it. He'll get coffee at the office.

TWO

THE PARKING LOT is already half-full with employee vehicles by the time Hunter makes it to work. He's often the first one in and the last to leave, but after the debacle with the coffee maker and Jillian's phone call, his motorcycle hadn't started and he'd had to take his truck. The rust-brown pick-up makes the fifteen-mile journey from his trailer to the airfield a lot slower than his bike.

As agitated as he is in the wake of his conversation with Jillian, he still can't help the smile on his face as walks into the SkyTrip hangar. He never had a kid, but he thinks he's had a fair approximation of fatherhood in getting SkyTrip off the ground. So to speak. There were a lot of growing pains to get it from the crazy idea stage to the going concern it is now, and he continues to be in awe of the fact that he's actually made a success of it.

Every time he takes one of their neat little Cessnas up in the air, leaving the desert by Joshua Tree far below and heads toward the washed out blue of the Southern

California sky, he allows himself to feel something he's hasn't felt often in his life. Pride. He can believe this hasn't all been a fluke, that he can have this—something that makes his life worth living. SkyTrip has been a shit-ton of work, but it's pretty much all that's kept him sane these last few years.

He hasn't done all that work alone, that's for sure. Hunter may have had the money, the life insurance that had sat untouched, growing interest, for ten years while he'd been in the Army and then trying to make it work with Jillian. Three years ago, it had all been a wild dream until a mutual friend put in him touch with Devin, and Devin had been, well, amazing. He'd been a rock and a cheerleader and the hardest worker Hunter's ever met. He loved Hunter's idea and even though he knew nothing about skydiving or airplanes or extreme tourism, he learned fast, and he'd been there for Hunter every step of the way.

Hunter's stomach flips uneasily when he spots Devin at his desk in the back, his short blond hair lit up like a halo by the industrial lighting. He's bent over his laptop, tapping away, occasionally stroking the short bordering-on-ginger beard that covers his angular chin. He's wearing his Pixies tee today, with a distinctly not-matching blue checkered short sleeved button-down over it. His uniform, in other words.

It's a familiar sight; when he's not working the mani-fest desk up front, dealing with customers in his charm-ingly British way that always puts the most nervous of them at ease, Devin's doing five things at once to keep this place running. Hunter doesn't know what he'd do without him. And he just told his ex-wife that he's bringing Devin as his date to her wedding. What on earth had possessed him to do that?

Process of elimination, he supposes, looking around the walled-off part of the hangar they use for office space and a break room. The SkyTrip team is small, and mostly taken. Louis, their chief mechanic and a pilot, was Hunter's second hire after Devin. He's fifty and in an on-again-off-again relationship with Tanya, the mother of their two teenage daughters. Will, a jumper who used to be in the Coast Guard, is closer to Hunter's age but still definitely in the sowing-wild-oats phase of his life. Isabelle's a jumper, too, plus a certified EMT, and not only would she laugh in Hunter's face if he asked her to pretend to be his girlfriend for a weekend, her wife would have some choice words to say about it, too. The last prospect, Laney, their only full-time pilot, might have done it. She's young, single, and straight. But Hunter didn't say her name. He said Devin's.

"Hey everyone," he says, taking off his aviators and sticking them in the vee of his white T-shirt. "Sorry I'm late."

"Bike trouble?" Louis asks.

"Yeah, had to take the truck in today. And I didn't have my coffee this morning, so let's make this meeting short, okay?"

At that, Devin raises his head from his screen, and pushes a cup of black coffee towards Hunter. He smiles his thanks and takes a sip of the brew; it's ten times better than he could have made at home even if the machine hadn't been on the fritz.

"What's our schedule today?"

Devin taps at his keyboard and gives them the rundown. "Newbie group in the first slot of the day. Tandem jumps. This afternoon, three solo jumps and our AFF class at four."

"Okay, great. How's the new helmet you've been trying?" Hunter asks Isabelle.

She gives him a concise summary of its pros and cons and finishes with, "I wouldn't order more until they fix the ventilation issue."

Hunter takes her at her word. "Devin, can you—"

"Notify the vendor we won't be ordering until they fix the ventilation issue? On it."

"Okay, that's everything for now, team. Stay safe."

The crew breaks up to finish prepping for their first run of the day. Hunter lingers by Devin's desk. He's not hiding behind his cup of coffee, he's just holding it as a bit of a security blanket.

"What?" Devin says. He's barely looked up from his computer all morning. Maybe Hunter's been working him too hard. Maybe he owes him a vacation. In upstate New York.

"So, remember when I told you Jillian was getting married again?"

Devin lifts his head and takes his fingers off his keyboard, peering at Hunter with eyes the same color as the fuselage of his first plane—a flat gray blue.

"Yeah," he says cautiously.

"Can you make sure my schedule's clear?" Hunter does a mental face palm. How chicken shit is he going to be about this? "Actually, I was hoping, if you don't have other plans that weekend, that maybe you'd like to take a few days off and come with me. To the wedding. Keep me company."

Devin's expression changes from wary to baffled. "What?"

"You haven't taken any time off in a while and it's really beautiful up there and I think you said one time you'd always wanted to visit the Finger Lakes, which are really close to where the wedding's going to be. And you know I don't even really want to go, but Jillian—well, I have to. I know I'm not making it sound like much fun, but I promise it will be."

"You want me to go on vacation with you to the Finger Lakes to your ex-wife's wedding?"

Hunter hasn't thought this through even a little bit. He nods.

Devin drags the moment out a beat longer, then shrugs as if he gets weirder requests on a daily basis. "You're paying for the plane tickets. Business class. At least."

Hunter's nod gets faster. "Of course. Only fair." He feels something in his chest lighten with Devin's agreement. Jillian's wedding will be way more fun with Devin there. Most things are. "Awesome. Cool." He notices the time, knows he's going to have to hustle to get ready for the first group of the day. "Oh and—"

"Don't worry, I'll book the tickets." Devin shakes his

head, affecting an air of being put upon, but Hunter sees right through him.

"Thanks." He grins, and Devin smiles back. Okay, that could have gone worse. He still has to think of a way to explain the fact that Jillian thinks they'll be attending as a couple. But that's a problem for another day.

THREE

DEVIN HAS BEEN WELL aware that Hunter's ex-wife is getting married. Hunter isn't the chattiest guy in the world, but of everyone at SkyTrip, Devin's known him the longest and as such, is the least intimated by him. Devin knows he can say pretty much anything to Hunter, and he hopes that Hunter feels the same way about him. So yeah, he's known about Jillian's upcoming wedding to fellow doctor Aaron Something-or-Other for a while. He even knew that Hunter was invited. To Devin, whose parents have been married, divorced, married other people, divorced them, then married each other *again*, relationships are an elastic concept you don't do well to put into predetermined boxes. Hunter and Jillian keep in touch, and Hunter is wanted at the wedding. Well, all right then.

But it was not on Devin's radar that Hunter might actually attend. He's cutting it fine, with their slots at SkyTrip usually booked weeks in advance, Devin's going to have to do some fancy scheduling magic to make sure all their bookings are covered while Hunter is out of town. Devin can make it happen, but it would have been easier if Hunter had blocked out the time a month or two ago.

However, not even in Devin's wildest fancies had it occurred to him that Hunter might want Devin to accompany him to said wedding. What could Hunter have been thinking of? And what had Devin been thinking when he'd said he'd go?

It's not like they aren't friends. They very much are, born out of their business partnership, a partnership that will soon be inked into legally binding format as soon as they get the official papers back from SkyTrip's attorney. But they aren't the kind of friends who go on holiday together. Hunter hasn't taken off more than a weekend in the three years since they opened SkyTrip. Devin hasn't taken much more than that. Honestly, they could both use a break.

So if Hunter wants Devin to come with him in order to take a vacation, then far be it from Devin to say no. It might be nice, at that, to spend some time together outside of work. Yes, the circumstances are bit ridiculous, but people do weird things when their exes get remarried. His mother dyed her hair purple when his father married Sylvie, and his dad broke two fingers punching a hole through a wall when his mother married Jim. If that's not true love, Devin doesn't know what is.

The arrangements are made. SkyTrip will have to survive without them for four days. They have two connecting flights, from Palm Springs to Denver, Denver to Albany. The planes are too small for first class, but

Devin happily pays the premium for business class with Hunter's card. On travel day Devin locks up his apartment and goes to pick Hunter up in his fuel-efficient compact because Hunter's truck doesn't have air conditioning and Devin refuses to ride all the way to the Palm Springs airport in ninety-degree heat sweating like a glass of iced tea.

Devin's kind of looking forward to the trip, truth be told. He's not the greatest flyer, but he has a pharmacopoeia of herbal remedies in case his anxiety becomes too much. Once at their destination, he'll get to relax for a few days in rural New York state with his best friend. Plus, he's not ashamed to admit he loves weddings. Free food and booze plus dancing and making small talk with strangers he'll never see again—what's not to like?

He puts his car into park outside of Hunter's trailer but leaves the engine, and thus the AC, on, and taps the horn. He doesn't have to wait long before his boss-slash-best-friend appears, juggling a backpack, a duffle bag, and a half-eaten apple. It's ungodly early, but Hunter looks alert, his longish so dark as to be almost black hair swept back from his squarely handsome face, his sunglasses hooked into the top of his white tee shirt. He quickly stows his bag in the boot next to Devin's wheely suitcase the drops into the passenger seat, slamming the door shut behind him. He's not a large man, but he fills the little car up with his presence anyway.

"Ready to go?" Hunter asks, or that's at least what Devin thinks he says because his mouth is full of half-chewed apple.

Devin pulls away from the curb and heads for the

highway to Palm Springs. "Ready as I'll ever be. Coffee in the holder there."

"Oh thank god." Hunter swallows his last bite of apple. The core goes into the bin bag Devin keeps behind the driver's seat and Hunter takes a big gulp from the travel cup Devin filled at home. The cold air pouring from the vents pushes the scent of coffee and Hunter's deodorant into Devin's face.

He glances over. Hunter's looking at him, an odd crease in his forehead. "What?"

"Just wanted to thank you for going with me," Hunter says. "And there's something I haven't told you. Well, something I need to tell you."

Devin's gut squirms at that. He can't help his mind from going into impossible directions with what Hunter might mean. "Go on, then."

"Thanks for driving, by the way."

Devin shrugs. "Not a problem."

"You're a better driver than me," Hunter says.

Devin's eighty percent sure Hunter's stalling, but he takes the bait anyway. "I am?"

"You're very...conscientious. I always feels safe when I ride with you." And then Hunter smiles at him.

Devin belies his safety-conscious reputation for a moment as he lets his eyes linger on Hunter's smile instead of on the road. He knows that Hunter would never, could never, return Devin's long-hidden affections, but that doesn't stop his heart from flip-flopping in his chest whenever Hunter smiles. It's not fair that his smile is up there with the all-time greats.

"Oh, shit." Hunter's smile drops.

Devin returns his gaze to the road now that the dazzle of Hunter's smile is gone. "What is it?"

"I forgot to tell you about the dress code. The wedding—we're supposed to wear suits and ties. I forgot to tell you to get a suit."

"*Get* a suit? You think I don't own a suit?" Devin does a very good approximation of insulted.

"Well, considering that I've never seen you dressed in anything other than jeans and the same seven band shirts with short sleeved button-downs...yeah."

Devin refrains from looking down at his outfit. Short sleeved button-downs suit the climate they live in, and he likes this Radiohead shirt. "Don't worry. I've got a suit, and I even packed it." He had, in fact, already had it hanging in his closet, but it had been a while, his parents' most recent wedding, since he'd worn it. "Besides, you should talk. Do you own anything besides white T-shirts, jeans, and your leather jacket?"

Hunter scoffs. "I have a suit," he says grumpily.

"Please tell me it's not the suit you married Jillian in, because that would just be weird."

Hunter laughs at that. Devin tries to keep the smile off his own face. He loves being able to make Hunter laugh.

"No, it's not," Hunter says, trying to sound superior and failing. "It's older than that. Hope it still fits. Maybe I should have gotten something new."

"We'll take a look when we get there, see what's what," Devin says briskly. He may not be a fashion icon, but he knows what looks good. Of course, on Hunter, that would be anything, including a paper bag.

"You take good care of me," Hunter says.

Devin lets the glow of pleasure from that reside pathetically in his chest for a moment before sweeping the feeling away. *Not allowed, Devin.* "So, what was it that you needed to tell me before?"

Hunter shifts in his seat. Is he nervous?

"Oh. Right. Just in case Jillian mentions it or asks or something, she kind of thinks you're coming with me to the wedding as my date. Because we're dating."

"We are?" Devin says blankly, feeling as if he's missed a step the size of a staircase.

"She really wanted me to bring someone, and I sort of told her you'd be my date. I'm sorry.

Hunter sounds contrite. "It was a weird impulse and I'll tell her that we're only friends when we get there. Sorry. I'm an idiot."

"Well, we're in agreement there," Devin says lightly. The randomness of Hunter asking him to accompany him gets slightly less random. "Look, it's fine. I don't know why it's so important to your ex-wife that you have a date to her wedding, but if it helps you out...." Devin trails off, because he's not exactly sure what he's agreeing to. In his most honest moments, after a pint or two or when sobbing his way through his umpteenth viewing of *Sense and Sensibility* and despairing of ever finding his own Colonel Brandon, he knows he'd do literally anything Hunter Pike asked him, up to and including jumping out of an airplane thousands of feet above the earth. He'd never ask him that, but still. Pretending to be his boyfriend for a few days isn't so bad, in the big scheme of things, not if it helps Hunter out. Even if Devin's heart might be a bit battered by the end of it when they come home and everything goes back to normal.

"Really? You'd do that for me?"

I'd do anything for you. Devin bites back the words. "Sure, mate. If that's going to make this easier all around," he says instead, trying to keep his voice neutral. "We're partners, aren't we?"

"That's right." Hunter smiles again and Devin represses his impulse to sigh like an infatuated teenager. "Thanks, Devin. I'll make it up to you somehow. I'll buy you a bottle of Dewar's at the airport."

Devin sniffs ostentatiously. "Well, it's a start anyway."

Hunter laughs and the glow behind Devin's ribs is back. He is in so much trouble.

FOUR

HUNTER WASN'T LYING about Devin being a better driver than he is. He tends toward impatient, wanting to scoot around law abiding citizens who follow the speed limit. Hence the motorcycle. But Devin, while not staid, seems to be able to carry on a conversation, keep up with the flow of traffic, and obey all the posted signs simultaneously and seemingly effortlessly. He's driving them in their rental vehicle, an unexceptional gray SUV, to their first destination of this destination wedding: the house Jillian grew up in, the one her parents still live in.

"And the wedding's the day after tomorrow?" Devin asks.

"Late afternoon. At Atkins Farm. It used to be a dairy, now it's an events venue, I guess." He remembers the rich earthy scent of manure announcing the dairy miles before the red-on-white hand painted sign pointing the way.

"And you grew up here, too?" Devin asks, waving vaguely to the landscape zipping by the SUV's windows.

They've left the capitol city and the suburbs behind and are in true rural upstate New York now. It's not all farms, but there are still a few, broken up every few miles by a small town center, and in between lots and lots of trees.

"Guilty," Hunter says. "Jillian and I went to high school together, believe it or not."

Devin looks surprised, even behind his sunglasses. The solstice is just past, and the days are still long. The area's having a seasonably warm stretch, complete with humidity. "I didn't realize you'd known her that long."

"Since we were kids, actually." He wonders that he's never told Devin any of this before, but then most of their conversations since they met have been about SkyTrip. At first it was how to get it started, then how to make it profitable, and lately it's been about how to make it sustainable. Hunter never thought he'd be cut out to last in any job for more than a few years— even in the army he wasn't happy unless he was moving around, learning something new. But SkyTrip is different. It's his. His and Devin's. And he can't imagine himself doing anything else.

"First love?" Devin asks. He's using the deceptively soft voice he uses when he wants a deal from a supplier and he's not going to relent until he gets it. "After all, if you're dragging your new beau to your ex's wedding, it's only fair I be prepared."

Hunter winces. All day he's managed to stuff that wrinkle to the back of his mind, pretending that he and his best friend are just taking a trip to another friend's wedding, not that sticky little triangle he managed to tangle them up in where Devin's going to pretend to be—

Hunter's brain can't even imagine what it is that Devin's going to pretend to be. His date, sure. But what does that mean? Will they pretend to be together, like in a relationship? Will they pretend to be in love? Jillian's going to see through them the second she meets Devin, anyway, so he doesn't even know why he's going to try.

Her soft, almost pitying voice, though, the other day on the phone. She's *worried* about him and it makes him feel—

"Hunter, you okay?" Devin asks.

Hunter realizes his hands are balled into fists and he hasn't responded to Devin's perfectly reasonable question. He's the one who dragged Devin all the way across the country when he knows perfectly well Devin's not the best flyer, though he didn't seem too bad on their flights today, but maybe that had to do with the CBD gummy bears he was chewing like, well, candy. The least he can do is give him some background on what they're heading into.

"First love? I guess you could call it that. She's a couple of years younger. Like you. We lived on the same street; our parents were friends. It wasn't like we were betrothed from birth or anything, but they were happy when I finally noticed the skinny girl I'd grown up having water balloon fights with in the summer and going ice skating with in the winter had grown up. She was smart— way smarter than me, and so pretty. I was senior when she finally just told me I should kiss her, or she was going to ask Tyler Jenkins to the winter formal instead of me." Hunter smiles, remembering their awkward, chaste first kiss. His first. Probably not hers. He got the hang of it pretty fast, though.

"We dated until I left for college, but we stayed in touch. And then my parents died." He rubs his sternum to quell the pain that flares up whenever he thinks of them, soldiers on. "I quit school, joined the Army, and one day a few years later I was on leave and she was almost done with med school and we just—we had this whirlwind reconnection that ended with me proposing to her on the roof of the hospital where she was doing her rotation and we got married that night. We were together for two years of mostly long distance until she pulled the plug."

He knew it wasn't going to work from practically the day after their impromptu elopement. He'd been due back at the base, she had board exams. They didn't have room for each other in their lives, but he'd been so desperate to have something good, something that would give him a reason to come back from the dark, violent places the Army was sending him and his special ops team. Still— "It was a relief when she told me she was filing the papers. Six months later I got discharged and a few months after that I met you for coffee because Ted Buckley told me you were someone who knew about numbers and computers and things." He glances over at Devin, who takes a right onto Apple Vale's main artery without consulting the GPS. How does he do that? They're almost there.

Devin hasn't reacted to this Reader's Digest version of the Hunter and Jillian story. Hunter doesn't know what he hoped he'd say, but he's not expecting what comes out of Devin's mouth.

"Ted told me he had a friend who needed a reality check. I think he was hoping I'd talk you out of the idea of opening your own skydiving school."

"Seriously?"

"Instead, you talked me into it, with your passion and your teeth."

He laughs. "My teeth? What did they have to do with anything?"

"You've got this All-American smile. I knew if we could put that smile on the adverts, we'd be millionaires."

"Not quite millionaires," Hunter says. "But at least we're in the black."

"Thanks to me," Devin says.

"Entirely thanks to you," he agrees. They've passed the quaint downtown and are already in the leafy outskirts of town. The McVays' traditional two-story colonial looms on the corner of Elm and Bayberry. Half a dozen cars are parked out front. "We're here."

Devin parallel parks without fuss, shuts off the engine. "You ready?"

Hunter swallows down his discomfort. He's jumped out of airplanes hundreds of times, some of those times into active war zones. Having dinner at his ex-in-laws with his ex-wife should be a piece of cake. "Sure." He's trying for breezy, but the word comes out more like a croak.

Suddenly there's a warm hand on his knee. He glances down. Devin gives him a reassuring pat before he withdraws. "Look, the good news is, I'm great with parents. Let me be my delightful self and you just smile and nod. And if it's too much, you say the word and we'll get out of here. All right?"

Hunter attempts to follow what Devin's saying, but he's still processing the residual warm pressure on his knee for some reason. He must be more tired from the flights than he thought if he's getting so thrown off by a simple friendly touch. "What word?" Hunter asks finally.

"What, like a code word? Yeah, good idea," Devin says without Hunter having to explain himself. He hums in thought for a moment. "Like 'duct tape.'"

"Duct tape?" Hunter repeats uncomprehendingly.

"Yeah, you say duct tape and we split. Okay?"

"Uh. Okay."

"It's going to be fine, Hunter, I promise." Devin takes his sunglasses off and tucks them into the pocket of his over shirt. Hunter notices that his blue-gray eyes look particularly bright as his irises shrink in the late afternoon light. He takes a deep breath. He has Devin on his side. He can do this. And if he can't, well, all he has to say is duct tape.

FIVE

DEVIN'S never met Hunter's ex-wife, but he's prepared to hate her a little, on principle. He's seen Jillian's picture, a framed snapshot on Hunter's desk, from which he knows she's got an open-faced beauty, all straight white teeth and straighter brown hair. She's a pediatric oncologist, the kind of doctor you go to when your kid might have cancer. The kind no one wants to see. She's always loomed in Hunter's past as this more-perfect-than-perfect figure. Hunter always talks about her fondly, and Devin knows they keep in touch more frequently than the average divorced couple. Not that Devin's jealous.

He wonders if in his assumed role as Hunter's love interest a little jealousy would be allowed.

It's all moot anyway because the woman who opens the door isn't Jillian. She's a tall, late middle-aged woman with chicly cut gray hair. Her smile warms the severe lines of her face.

"Hunter, my darling, you look fabulous, come in, and this must be Devin, so very pleased to meet you, I'm

Myrna, Jillian's mother." As she ushers them in, Hunter pauses to give her a hug and a kiss on the cheek. Devin's a little surprised at the display of physical affection—he's never witnessed Hunter be particularly touchy feely. He follows them into the foyer. It's a large house, not newly built but obviously well cared for. A huge bouquet of periwinkle hydrangeas sits on an attractive table near the base of a wide staircase, and there's an old-fashioned coat rack in one corner. In this gleaming home, Devin feels his trip-related grubbiness more acutely, but Myrna doesn't seem to mind them being road-weary. She keeps up a stream of conversation as they pass through the living room, where a distracted-looking blond woman is playing blocks with a little boy, then into the kitchen, where a catering crew is setting up the evening meal.

"We're eating on the patio. It's just family tonight," Myrna says. "I'll get you something to drink. Wine?"

"Just water for me," Hunter says.

"Of course, you've just flown all day, you must be dehydrated." Myrna edges her way around the workers in the kitchen and takes a pitcher of water from the refrigerator. Everything in this house is old—no, not old, classic. Including Myrna herself. She's got the name of a Hollywood star and she carries herself like one, upright and patrician. She's formidable. No wonder Hunter was a little apprehensive about seeing his in-laws again.

Ex-in-laws, Devin reminds himself.

Glasses of cool water in hand, Myrna shows them where they can freshen up, and then tells them everyone else is gathered on the back patio.

"Who's everyone?" Devin asks.

"Gary, my husband. Jillian's brother, that's his girl-friend Anna in the living room with their son, Kai. And Aaron's mother—his father passed away a few years ago. A few more cousins from our side of the family will be here by dinner time."

"And Jillian?" Hunter asks. He sounds normal, relaxed, even, but the muscles around his mouth are tense.

"Oh, they're out meeting with the wedding planner at the farm, but they should be back soon." Myrna pauses at the French door to the patio and grabs Hunter's hand, the one not holding the glass of water. "She is so happy that you're here, Hunter. And so am I. It's really wonderful to see you."

They hold eye contact for a moment, then Myrna clasps Hunter's hand and lets it drop. Devin thinks he sees a tear forming in the corner of her eye, but she blinks it away and opens the door.

Hunter gives him a sort of sad smile as they follow Myrna outside. Devin shakes his head. If Myrna is any indication, Hunter really doesn't have anything to worry about. He's like the prodigal son returning home, and he's being welcomed with open arms. Literally, in fact, as they approach the group standing around a flagstone patio in the lovely big backyard. There's a grill, not in use at the moment, and a couple of big patio tables, and even a pool set a way back from the house. Jillian's parents seem quite well-off. Hunter said they lived down the road from each other. He wonders if where Hunter grew up was a posh as this.

A stocky man with a full head of gray hair opens his

arms and wraps Hunter in a bear hug. Devin grabs Hunter's glass before it smashes all over the flagstone.

"Hunter, my boy, it's been too long."

"Hi, Gary," Hunter says warmly. "Staying out of trouble?"

"I try." Gary laughs, booming and jolly. "No promises, though."

Myrna rolls her eyes at her husband in a practiced motion of someone who's been married decades. Devin recognizes the attitude from his own parents' exasperated affection for each other.

"I'm going to check on the caterers. We'll be sitting down to eat in about half an hour, okay?" Myrna disappears into the house without waiting for an answer.

Gary smiles at Devin and glances at Hunter, but he doesn't begin the introductions, so Devin offers his hand. "I'm Devin Smith."

Gary's answering shake is firm. "Gary McVay. Welcome to Apple Vale."

Hunter looks like he's having trouble getting words out, so Devin merely says, "Nice to meet you." A skinny young man with a light brown goatee joins the group and claps Hunter on the back. This must be Jillian's brother. He asks if Hunter's still jumping out of planes.

"Every day, Rick."

"Awesome. You jump, too?" Rick asks, nodding at Devin.

"Not if my life depended on it," Devin says with feeling, which makes the crowd laugh. He relaxes a degree and turns to meet the last in the little party, an attractive middle-aged woman with dark hair who Gary introduces as Delphina, Aaron's mother, in town from Washington D.C. where she's an immigration lawyer.

"You want to see my green card?" Devin jokes. "I think I left it in my other jacket."

"I'm not that kind of immigration lawyer," she reassures him. "At the moment I'm advocating for unaccompanied minors who cross the southern border."

Devin feels like an ass for joking over his immigration status, which is far more secure than many, but Delphina doesn't seem to hold it against him. Instead, they make small talk about D.C. since Devin lived there for a few months when he first came to the States, following a guy who turned out not to have been worth the trouble. He fell out of love with the guy but in love with America.

"I never knew you lived in D.C.," Hunter says, apparently following the conversation between Delphina and Devin while talking to Rick and Gary about something completely different.

"There's a lot you don't know about me," Devin replies a little saucily, because that's what he'd do if he was properly dating Hunter. His tone apparently throws Hunter off, because he chokes on a sip of water. Devin reaches over to pat his back lightly, then looks around for a tissue or a napkin or something.

"I'm fine," Hunter reassures him. Devin drops his hand from between Hunter's shoulder blades, pretends not to notice how firm and warm beneath the cotton tee.

Delphina smiles at them. "How long have you two been together?"

Hunter coughs again and Devin internally sighs. They probably should have worked out some of these details ahead of time, but Hunter hadn't brought it up and Devin certainly wasn't going to press him on creating the fake history of their fake relationship. This is weird enough. Still, Devin promised he would do his best. He puts on his most charming smile.

"Well, we've known each other for over three years now, since SkyTrip was just a twinkle in Hunter's eye," he says. That's true enough.

"That's your skydiving school? How terribly exciting every day must be," Delphina says, sounding sincerely interested.

"It has its moments," Devin agrees. There was the time one of the engines on the Cessna cut out and Laney had to do an emergency landing on a desert highway. Or the time Hunter's first chute didn't deploy. He calmly executed backup protocol and the second one was fine. Devin lost a year off his life when Hunter told the story after the fact, but honestly, he didn't worry about Hunter up in the air. He was more likely to wreck his motorcycle getting to and from work than having an accident up in the sky, where they double and triple checked everything every day.

"So, it was love at first sight, then?" Delphina presses. Damn lawyers and their tenacity.

Devin lets out a nervous chuckle. On his part, very nearly. He'd been in a Santa Monica Starbucks waiting to meet the guy his friend Ted said needed some business advice. Since getting his MBA, Devin had been involved in several startups, getting their business licenses set, setting up LLCs, payroll systems and the like. Ted said this Hunter Pike fellow wanted to start a skydiving school, and maybe Devin could talk some sense into him.

Devin hadn't known what to expect from someone whose name alone made him sound like an adrenaline junky, but then this beautiful man had walked into the Starbucks and taken his breath away. His dark brown, almost black hair was long, falling over his brow and ears. His body was compact, but he looked like he knew what to do with it. He obviously worked out; his solid chest was encased in a tight plain white t-shirt. The well-fitting jeans, heavy black boots, and—naturally—aviator sunglasses all combined to make him look more like an action movie star than a skydiving addict.

By that point, Devin had lived in Los Angeles for five years. He was used to seeing beautiful people. He'd even seen his share of actual movie stars, who, it turned out, were just humans who wanted to walk their dogs and buy overpriced kombucha and get In N Out like everyone else. But he'd never gotten a physical jolt of want when he'd seen Ben Affleck at the Hollywood Farmer's Market or John Boyega at the Arclight theater. This man was different. Devin wanted him from the very first.

He ordered a coffee, looked around the small shop, then spotted Devin. He'd taken off his aviators, looked at Devin with his lichen green eyes, and smiled. And oh, that smile, his secret weapon. It was massively unfair to release it on a twenty- nine-year-old gay British expat whose last relationship had ended three months earlier. Especially when Adam was still kipping on Devin's couch because he hadn't had a music gig in a while; Devin was getting sick of dating his right hand.

"Devin Smith?" the beautiful man had asked.

"Hunter Pike?" Devin had said, or he must have done, because the man nodded and sat down across from him and told him about his dream of opening a skydiving school, of all things. And a month later, Devin had moved himself to the desert a hundred and fifty miles east of that coffee shop, leaving his life in L.A. behind to help Hunter open SkyTrip.

Love at first sight? More like love at first smile.

But Hunter's not smiling now.

"Not exactly," Devin says, answering Delphina's question. "More like a work friends turned um, benefits, thing?" He glances at Hunter, nudges his boot with his sneakered toe.

Hunter jumps and adds, "We spend so much time together at work, it just kind of...happened."

Delphina looks slightly disappointed at this answer.

Devin breaks in. "Ever the romantic, isn't he?"

"Hunter, a romantic?" A new voice enters the conversation. "He's a soft center in a crusty exterior."

"A bit like a good sourdough bread," Devin quips. He turns to meet the new arrival who seems so sure of Hunter's nature. He places the girl-next-door good looks immediately. Jillian.

SIX

"HI JILLIAN," Hunter says, voice low and warm as he hugs his ex-wife. Devin doesn't have time to feel much of anything, not jealousy, not concern, because then Jillian's hugging *him*. She's got strong arms and smells like lavender.

"It is so fantastic to finally meet you, Devin," she says. She sounds, improbably, like she means it. "I've heard so much about you and I could not be happier to have you here."

As greetings to one's ex's supposed significant other go, it's a generous one. Devin finds himself smiling in response. "You're too kind to have us," he says. "And congratulations."

"Thanks." She gives him one more squeeze, then brings a tall man with neatly combed brown hair into the circle of the group. "Devin, Hunter, this is Aaron Garza."

"Aaron." Hunter nods and shakes his hand, much cooler to him than he'd been with Jillian. Devin wants to roll his eyes at Hunter's transparency, but he supposes he has a right. He makes his own greeting noticeably warmer.

"Aaron, it's a pleasure. We've already gotten to know your delightful mother," Devin says.

"Thanks for coming guys." Aaron either doesn't notice Hunter's coolness or doesn't care. He grins at them and puts his arm around Jillian's waist in a casual gesture that seems authentic rather than territorial.

Devin finds himself shifting closer to Hunter, mirroring the closeness of the other couple. He doesn't touch, though. This farce isn't an excuse for him to indulge in every passing inclination to put his hands on Hunter, to brush his hair away from his forehead, to feel the muscles shift and move under his shirt. This isn't Devin-gets-what-he-wants day.

He keeps half an eye on Hunter as they all chat about the wedding, but he seems to be coping. He's already come up with three excuses he could make to jet out of there if Hunter gives him the signal, but then Myrna calls them all to the tables for the meal and Hunter doesn't hesitate before heading over with the rest of the group.

It's a rush of people and voices and confusion and Devin gets a pang of homesickness for his family gatherings back home. His parents are each one of four siblings, so he has the attendant number of aunts, uncles, cousins, cousins by marriage and so on. He hasn't been home in a few years, and he suddenly wishes he hadn't stayed away so long. SkyTrip had needed him. Hunter had needed him. But he's beginning to realize that he's given everything to both Hunter and SkyTrip for so long, he's sort of forgotten to have a life of his own. Not that SkyTrip isn't his, too. He loves what he does, but if he hadn't met Hunter could he honestly say he'd be living in a literal desert and running a skydiving school?

This situation just highlights how entwined in Hunter's life and goals he's gotten. He's here because Hunter asked him to be, because Hunter needs him. But not the way Devin needs Hunter.

His heart constricts uncomfortably. Perhaps when they get back from this silly wedding he needs to have a conversation with Hunter about the future. Because pining over his business partner for the rest of his life isn't exactly a sound plan.

In which case, this long weekend, in this beautiful place, surrounded by warm, friendly people, and with Hunter by his side—well, Devin's just going to have to make the most of it.

After a truly excellent meal of enchiladas and rice and beans and a fresh green salad, the sun's going down behind the trees on the edge of the yard. Jillian and Aaron can't stop smiling—at this rate they'll be exhausted before they get to the actual wedding reception in two days' time. Rick and Anna's little one has climbed into Myrna's lap and is sucking his thumb adorably. Devin's always liked kids, as long as he can give them back to their proper owners after a while.

Hunter seems relaxed and is talking to Gary about some old airfield on the edge of town that's fallen into disrepair.

Jillian catches his eye during a break in conversation. "Have you two checked into your hotel yet?"

Devin blinks. "Uh, no. Motel, I think, someplace on

Route 20? By the time we booked there was nothing closer."

"Don't be silly, you two are staying here," Myrna says.

"Oh, well, gosh— "

"The guest room is all made up and it has its own bathroom." Her tone doesn't invite refusal, but Devin's not sure. He's sort of been banking on them being able to call off the fake relationship thing when they're in private. But there won't be any privacy, not if they stay here. In the guest room. With its presumable guest bed. Singular.

He glances at Hunter, whose mouth is sealed into a line. Devin can read his micro-expressions as if he'd been programmed with some Hunter Pike translation program at birth, so he can tell Hunter wants to give in and accept. It would be more convenient to be right in town instead of driving to and from their out-of-the-way motel, anyway.

"Of course," he says before Hunter can answer. "Thank you so much for offering. I'll go call and cancel the room right now." He'd reserved rooms, plural, but no one here needs to know that.

"Thanks, Myrna," Hunter says. He doesn't make eye contact with Devin. Great. Devin-doesn't-get-what-he-wants day continues.

SEVEN

IT'S BEEN a long time since Hunter's had to talk to so many people, to put on such a relentlessly happy face. Sure, he talks to people every day at work, but that's a practiced spiel, his safety lessons, his pep talks for those who find their courage depleted at 10,000 feet. Work is work. Making small talk with Jillian's family is different. He's out of practice. Thank god for Devin.

His friend is right this minute on his hands and knees on the living room rug making a tower of blocks with toddler Kai, who laughs and claps delightedly every time the tower wobbles precariously. Hunter's never seen Devin around a child. Louis's girls are teenagers, they don't count. It's a surprisingly sweet sight. He blinks and turns away, sensing Jillian at his elbow.

"You okay?" she whispers. She's been nothing but smiles all night, but now she's got her concerned face on.

"Yeah, I'm good, Jill."

"Aaron likes you."

"Aaron likes everyone," he returns. He hadn't been surprised at how well they look together, Jillian and Aaron, the golden couple, even though they are both dark-haired, they glow with a sort of beatific light. Aaron recently came back from a stint abroad for Doctors Without Borders and is now doing ER work at Jillian's hospital in the Bronx.

"Go where I'm needed, that's what I do," he'd said earlier that night, and you'd think with lines like that he'd be a smug douchebag but he's actually nice, which is almost worse. Hunter shouldn't not like the guy, it's obvious that he makes Jillian happy, but he supposes there's some lizard brain part of him that will never fully be comfortable with the man who's succeeding in giving Jillian the love and life she deserves where Hunter failed so miserably.

"Well, that's true," Jillian agrees easily. "Aaron does like everyone, including you. I think he was a little nervous to meet you. But you've been on your best behavior."

"Were you worried?"

"A little. I thought maybe you wouldn't show," she admits. Her gaze flicks over to Devin. The block tower is about to fall. "But you did. And I finally got to meet Devin."

Her tone gives nothing away, but Hunter knows there's a question in there somewhere, one he doesn't want to answer.

"I'm really happy for you, Jill," he says, and he leans over to press a soft kiss to her cheek.

When he pulls away, he looks back to the block

tower. Devin's eyes are on him, but they cut away quickly.

"Are *you* happy, Hunter?" she asks. "Because that's all I ever wanted."

He doesn't know how to answer the question. He knows it's important to her, that he be happy, that he move on. That's why he's here, to prove how fucking happy he is to see his ex-wife make a life with someone else. He sighs. He is, though, is the thing. It's not like he still wants her. It's not like they made any sense, really, after high school. He was clinging to the only shred of his past that didn't make him feel like shit, and she was trying to save him.

"I'm happy for you," he says again. "And I'm working on the rest, okay?"

She searches his face with her gaze for a long moment. "Okay. I think—I think he's good for you."

His eyes widen. He almost asks who, but then he remembers. Devin, of course. He feels a stab of guilt that he's lied to her, and that he's putting Devin through this, and something else—something like wistfulness that he's never going to find someone who makes him happy the way Aaron make Jillian happy. Then there's a crash and a bang as the wooden block tower topples and scatters everywhere across the rug. Kai giggles uncontrollably as Devin makes an exaggerated reaction to the fallen tower. Hunter takes a step toward the mess when Jillian speaks.

"Goodnight, Hunter. We'll see you tomorrow."

"You aren't staying here?"

"No, we're at the inn downtown. Rick and Anna and

Kai are in the downstairs suite, though. So keep it down tonight." Then she winks and is gone.

Hunter shakes his head. He had been torn about Myrna's offer, on the one hand knowing it made their fake-dating thing more complicated, on the other, not wanting to disappoint the woman who'd been as much of a mother to him as his own. Devin had smoothly accepted, making things easier on him, like he'd been doing all day. Hunter owes him big time. He can start to repay the huge debt he's racking up by helping clean up a few blocks.

It's not late if he does the math and figures they're still on California time, but he's still yawning hugely by the time they say goodnight to the rest of the household, Kai having long since been put to bed by his parents. He and Devin get their bags from the rental car, then climb the wide staircase to the second floor. The master suite is on one side of the landing, on the other are two rooms on opposite sides of the hall each with their own bathroom. One of the rooms used to be Jillian's and has since been turned into a study for Gary, lined with bookshelves and containing a napping couch and a rowing machine. Hunter suspects the couch gets far more action than the rowing machine does.

The second bedroom used to be Ricky's, but sometime in the last few years Myrna and Gary replaced the BMX bike posters and drum kit with tastefully generic watercolors on the walls and blonde wood furniture. The dominant feature of the room is the big bed centered on the wall. It's got a crisp light blue comforter and white sheets, like a hotel. Back home, Hunter's trailer is on the small side; he's only got a double. He's never seen Devin's bedroom. He wonders for a moment what Devin wears to bed. Hunter's standard pajamas are a pair of boxer briefs. It's hot in the desert.

Okay, he really hasn't thought this guest room thing through.

"I'm sorry, again."

"For what?" Devin doesn't look at him, or at the bed, just sets his suitcase down on the floor and unzips it.

"I mean, where do I start?"

"Why don't you start with a shower?" Devin says briskly. "If we're going to be sharing a bed, I don't want to sleep next to all your airplane germs."

"I can sleep on the floor," Hunter offers. It's carpeted and there are plenty of pillows. God knows he slept in much worse conditions in the Army.

"Come on, I know we already established you're an idiot, but you can try to change. Go take your shower before I reconsider giving you first crack at the bathroom."

Hunter shrugs. Devin's kindness shouldn't surprise him after all this time, and it doesn't. But it is a surprise that Devin's still nice to *him*, especially after today. Someday he has a feeling he'll find out where Devin's tolerance for him ends and Hunter won't blame him one bit. Devin flipping out and demanding Hunter fix this situation would make a lot more sense to Hunter than this endless well of patience. Still, he doesn't want to find out Devin's limits tonight. He's too tired. So he does as he's told and goes to take a shower.

A few minutes later, the grime of travel washed away,

teeth clean, wearing a clean pair of underwear and a plain white undershirt, Hunter's back in the room. Devin's sitting on the edge of the bed, looking at his phone.

"Everything okay?"

"Pretty much. Just checking in with Isabelle and Will. Nothing came up today they couldn't handle. We've got an inquiry for a bachelor party for a couple of weeks from now, group of twelve. They want the Sky-High package."

Hunter runs the math in his head and whistles. The profit margin on their cushiest package will keep them in donuts for a couple of months at least. "Nice."

"Yeah, makes me think we should go on holiday more often." Devin taps a little more on his phone, then grabs a pile of his things off the bed and heads to the bathroom. "And I like the left side, by the way."

"It's all yours," Hunter says with a smile. Then the urge to apologize again becomes overwhelming. "Wait."

Devin stops just inside the bathroom door.

"You're making this really easy on me and I don't deserve it."

Devin looks like he's debating what to say. "It's okay. It's temporary, right?" And he closes the door between them before Hunter can reply.

It's easy to get settled in the queen bed, on the right side, of course. Hunter doesn't usually go to sleep this early if he considers the time change, but he's beat after the flights and the drive and the emotional minefield of being here, among these people. They all just seem to care about him so much, so happy to see him after so

many years away. That's why he's stayed away so long—
he doesn't deserve their unreserved love, as if he doesn't
have any blood on his hands, as if he still belongs in this
place, his hometown, as if it still belongs to him.

He's nearly asleep when the bed dips and Devin gets
in, turning off the light and making the room blessedly
dark.

"Hey Hunter," Devin whispers, as if they're
teenagers who don't want to wake the grownups down
the hall.

"Yeah, Devin?"

"You didn't say duct tape."

For a second Hunter doesn't know what he's talking
about, then remembers their half facetious code word.
He's just out of it enough to answer honestly. "I didn't
need to. You were there." Then he's asleep.

EIGHT

WHEN DEVIN OPENS his eyes the next morning, he's in bed alone. He sits up and checks his phone. It's well after nine. He rubs his eyes and checks again. How is it possible that he slept for almost ten hours? He's not a champion sleeper, rarely out for more than six or seven hours at the most. He chalks it up to the fatigue of travel, and the comfortable bed, much nicer than the rather unsupportive bed-in-box he'd ordered when he moved to the desert.

His dreams were a jumble of colors and people, but he remembers Hunter being in them, which is itself another oddity. He rarely remembers his dreams. Then again, the entire situation is odd. He'd been uncertain for about two seconds about sharing a bed with Hunter, but keeping things matter of fact seems to be working. If he reminds himself at regular intervals that this is all pretend and for Hunter's benefit, everything will be fine.

He does feel a bit guilty lying to all these nice people, people who seem to care very much for Hunter and his well-being. If he'd heard it once he'd heard it a dozen times: they're so happy to see Hunter, he'd stayed away too long, they're all dying to hear about his exciting life jumping out of airplanes attached to thrill-seeking bachelorettes or lawyers having a midlife crisis. If Hunter had worried about his reception, he clearly needn't have.

Devin dresses for what promises to be another warm, humid day, grabs his phone from the charger, and heads downstairs. There's a pot of coffee in the kitchen, and a plate of what appears to be peach-poppy-seed muffins, so Devin helps himself to both, then wanders outside to the backyard where Rick is chasing a giggling Kai around the yard. Myrna's on the phone and making notes on a pad of paper. She waves to him when she sees him. And Hunter —Hunter's in the pool.

Devin doesn't quite know if he's allowed to look, but he supposes he can't be blamed for the way his eyes keep sliding to the figure slicing through the water. Hunter's skin shows a definite farmer's tan, the strong arms several shades darker than his back, muscles rippling with every stroke. Hunter executes a perfect turn kick at the far end of the pool, then heads back toward Devin. He turns away abruptly before Hunter can see him watching, drops into a seat at the patio table next to Myrna.

"So you'll be there when the florist arrives. Perfect. Okay, see you then." She puts her phone down, makes another note on the pad, then gives Devin a broad smile. "Sleep well?"

"Like the proverbial baby," Devin says rather more heartily than warranted. Anything to distract him from the sight of a half-naked Hunter hauling himself out of the water, which he can tell is happening using his annoyingly good peripheral vision.

"Great. Well, we're unfortunately all busy with last minute wedding details, so you and Hunter are on your own for entertainment today, but we'll all meet at the venue for the rehearsal later."

"Anything we can help with?" Devin asks.

"You're sweet, but no. I have to rush now, but you two relax, enjoy yourself. If you don't have a swimsuit, you'll find spares in the downstairs guest bathroom. Help yourself."

"Yeah, you should come in, the water is amazing," Hunter says, suddenly next to Devin. He's dripping wet. Devin concentrates very hard on taking another sip of coffee. He's seen Hunter without a shirt on occasion, and those few times he'd tried desperately not to catalogue the ridges of his abdomen or notice the soft black hairs that cover his lower belly. But he's never seen so much of Hunter at once, in nothing but a pair of swim trunks that must be loaners because they hit Hunter mid-thigh. This is those few shirtless Hunter moments times ten. Maybe times a hundred. His thighs are thick and muscular, his ass round, his entire body solid and perfect. And it's all wet.

Devin swallows thickly, averts his eyes. "Um. You know I can't do anything before coffee."

"Right. Sorry. I woke up way too early, now I'm all wired." Hunter grabs a towel from a stack on the other patio table and wraps it around his middle before sitting in the chair next to Devin. Thank heaven for small mercies, now Devin only has to ignore a stunning set of shoulders and firm, flat pecs instead of the entire package. Bad choice of words as Devin wonders idly what the bulge inside those too-small trunks would look like in the open air.

"You didn't sleep well?" Devin asks to get his mind off the inappropriate visuals pinging around his brain.

"Actually, I slept so hard I didn't move until six, but once I opened my eyes, I couldn't get back to sleep."

"So, what are we going to do today? Myrna says we're not needed for wedding stuff."

"You are going to borrow a pair of swim trunks, and we are going in the pool. It's already getting humid. The swim will get your blood pumping. Then we'll get some lunch in town maybe? I haven't thought too far ahead. What do you want to do?"

Devin quite likes swimming, and it's not like he's hung up on the way he looks. He's fine, he works out regularly, keeps fit as any self-respecting man with a hopeless crush who's not actively dating would. But he's using all his self-control to get through this weekend as it is.

The refusal is on the tip of his tongue when Rick and Kai come up. "We're going in too, right, Kai Bear?" Rick says.

"Swimming!" Kai lisps. "Devin swim!"

"I'll get you a suit," Hunter says.

"No." Devin downs one more sip of coffee. "I brought my own. Give me ten minutes." It's hard to say who's smiling harder, the two-year-old or Hunter.

HUNTER'S STANDING in the shallow end, water up to his hip, encouraging Kai in his Paw Patrol water wings to scoot across the pool when the French door to the patio opens and Devin steps out. He's wearing his Green Day shirt today, but he's changed from jeans and sneakers into navy blue swim trunks and sandals. Hunter isn't sure he's ever seen Devin wear sandals before. And he's definitely never seen him in a swimsuit before. Not that that's relevant. He just wants Devin to enjoy this trip, to get some real vacation-type stuff in since Hunter's dragged him all this way to be his emotional support fake boyfriend.

He turns his attention to Kai, a preternaturally happy kid. Rick and Anna are doing a great job with him, according to Jillian, and Hunter has to agree. Rick was a bit of screwup back in the day, but he's since gotten his plumber's license and has a good job; he and Anna live a few towns over and are doing well. Hunter's never entertained the idea of having his own kid, but he hopes that Jillian and Aaron will take the plunge. She'll be a great mom, and Aaron seems like he'd be a great dad.

He's so focused on Kai's safety as the chubby little guy splashes and chases a hot pink floating duck around the shallow end that he misses Devin taking off his shirt and stepping out of his shoes; he suddenly gets splashed as Devin glides under the water near him, a ginger-blond fish kicking his way to the end of the pool. He swims back, stands up next to Hunter, water streaming off his body.

"Great idea, Hunter," Devin says. "The water feels really good."

"Good," Hunter echoes. His gaze is fully on Devin's

chest, which is as pale as the rest of him; Devin's always had a kind of stereotypically British complexion. But Hunter finds himself rather stupidly distracted by Devin's pecs. They're firm and well defined and he guesses he's never thought about what Devin might be covering up with those same seven band T-shirts. He knows his friend works out—they have the same interest in staying healthy, and there's a gym and a pool in Devin's apartment building. But man, he really didn't know how appealing Devin's slim hips, flat stomach, and strong shoulders would be unveiled all at once like this.

Or maybe it's just been too long since he's been with a guy and it's not that he's attracted to his best friend, because that would be—no, it's got to be that it's been a while for him. Still, he can't deny that he finds himself awkwardly semi-aroused, despite the cold pool water. What's the matter with him?

"What's up, Hunter?" Devin asks.

"Huh?"

"You just look a little...freaked out. You okay?"

He shakes his head, then spots something else. "Ah, just wondering about your tattoo. I didn't know you had one."

Devin turns to show off his left arm to Kai. "See, Devin's got a silly picture on his arm." He turns back around. "You didn't know that, Hunter?"

No, Hunter did not know that Devin had a tattoo, let alone one of a Tardis.

"I'm officially outed as the geek I am," Devin says ruefully. "Not like it was a big surprise."

"When did you get that?" Hunter asks. He stops himself from reaching out to trace the edges of the image.

"College, of course," Devin says. "Tequila may have been involved. Impressing a boy, as well."

"Dangerous combination," Hunter says. "Well, I like it."

Devin lifts his eyebrows. "Do you even know what it is?"

"Of course. I grew up on the '70s *Dr. Who*. Haven't seen as many of the newer seasons, but I liked David Tennant's doctor."

"Really?" Devin looks truly astonished. "He's my favorite."

"You have good taste," Hunter says.

"You have a secret nerdy side, color me impressed," Devin says, smiling lopsidedly.

Hunter's stomach does something weird at the sight of Devin's smile directed at him. Which makes no sense. Devin has smiled at him approximately infinity times over the past three years. Why would this time make Hunter feel something disturbingly close to a mix of nervous, giddy, and attracted that he hasn't experienced in so long he almost forgot what it felt like to—no. He's not *crushing* on Devin. That's the most ridiculous thought he's ever had, and he's had some doozies.

He tries to shake himself out of it as Devin takes over playing with Kai, swimming a few more laps to clear his head and cool himself down. The last thing he needs right now is to think their pretend relationship could be a real possibility.

NINE

WHEN DEVIN'S skin starts burning under the hot June sun and it's time for Kai's nap, they finally get out of the pool and take turns showering and changing. Hunter grabs the keys to the rental and keeps them on an almost frantic pace for the next few hours. First, it's lunch at a pleasant little cafe in the old-fashioned part of Apple Vale's fifties-era downtown followed by a tour of the area sights, such as they are.

Hunter drives by the high school he and Jillian attended and swings by the local ice rink where he learned to skate. He keeps up a very un-Hunter-like commentary on everything, and Devin soaks in every detail, forming a picture in his mind of Hunter as an adolescent, gifted at anything physical, school easy enough, too, but not necessarily a popular kid. It sounds like he didn't have many close friends, just teammates. And Jillian, of course.

Eventually they end up on the outskirts of town at the old airfield he remembers Gary mentioning last night.

Hunter pulls the SUV past the clearly empty office building and parks adjacent to the runway. Weeds grow up between the cracks in the asphalt. A medium-sized hangar with a corrugated tin roof squats off to the side. The whole operation is about a third of the size of SkyTrip.

They get out of the car and Hunter walks over to a bit of waist-high fencing, leans against it and stares off across the abandoned airfield. Devin leans against the fence, too, but his gaze is on Hunter.

"This is where I first learned to fly," Hunter says.

"How old were you?"

"First lesson? Ten, I think." He peers into the middle distance, as if he can see the ghosts of planes lifting off and setting down. "My dad taught me."

"Your dad was a pilot?" All Devin knows about Hunter's parents is that they're dead. He hasn't mentioned them once all day, even when telling Devin stories from his youth.

"He was. He was an older dad. He flew in Vietnam, met my mom when they got back. It took a few years to get pregnant with me. Only child, of course. She was a teacher but stopped when she had me. He kept a plane here, but he worked in an office, an insurance adjuster. He hated his job so much." Hunter shakes his head.

"But he loved to fly," Devin guesses.

"Boy, did he. My mom wasn't thrilled he started teaching me that young, but she saw how happy it made him. I was so excited, so happy to spend time with him. And the first time we took off and I was at the controls— oh my god, the complete rush of freedom, of just feeling like you're not tethered to the ground. That you've beat gravity, of all things."

Hunter looks like that little kid as he talks. His hair has fallen over his forehead again and Devin's fingers itch with wanting to comb it back. He wants to push Hunter against the fence and kiss him out here, under the June blue sky. But he stays put and listens to what Hunter's not saying.

"How did they die, Hunter?" he asks quietly.

"I was at college. Junior year. Trying to find myself, trying to figure out what to major in, and why I had a crush on my very male European History TA. Myrna was the one who called me. They'd gone out for a short flight over to Niagara and back—they used to do it all the time. But there was a lightning storm, and the instruments went out. Dad should have been able to manage, but they were over the Adirondacks. It was getting dark. They crashed about a hundred miles from here. Dead on impact."

Devin's beginning to see. "So you quit school and joined the Army."

"Would have done the Air Force, but Dad was Army. They have pilots, too."

"I'm so sorry, Hunter."

"The funny thing is, I never thought about signing up before. My dad would have hated it. It wasn't like I wanted to go to war or anything. But I was suddenly an orphan and school didn't make any sense anymore. I might have had a tiny death wish." The corners of his mouth turn down. "Only turns out, I was good at it. I took to it like a duck to water and I made special ops within three years. And that's when it got really—" Hunter takes a deep breath and Devin wants to tell him he doesn't have to keep going but he starts again "—scary. We saw some shit. We did...things. Things I'll never be able to talk about. But I got to fly. I learned to jump. And as amazing as it was the first time I took off in a plane, it doesn't compare to how it felt to jump out of one. The first time I did it solo—I thought, well, I seriously thought I might not pull my chute. I just wanted to keep falling."

Devin gives in then, puts a hand on Hunter's arm, squeezes. "I'm glad you pulled it." It's all he can think to say that isn't trite nonsense. It also happens to be true.

Hunter looks down at Devin's hand, then up to his face. His expression is unreadable. "I am, too. Everything that happened with Jillian, that was me trying to hang on to the part of me that decided to deploy my chute that day. She saved my life by giving me something to live for. But that, as we both found out, isn't the best basis for a healthy marriage."

"Do you still feel that way? When you jump?" Devin's not sure he wants to know the answer, but he has to ask.

Hunter's silent for a long moment. Then he says, " No. I don't. Mostly because I know you'll kill me if I end up dead."

It's a joke, but also not. Devin nods, takes his hand away. "Damn right I will."

Hunter laughs and some of the tension's broken, so Devin goes for it. "And what about your European History TA? Anything happen there?"

"Nah." His smile turns sly. "But the Army turned out to be a pretty good place to meet guys."

Devin lets out a shocked laugh. "Sometimes you do surprise me, Hunter Pike."

"What about you? To whom do you owe your sexual awakening?"

Devin lifts an eyebrow. He told Hunter he was gay at their very first meeting, just to get it out of the way, and Hunter had calmly replied that he was bi, and after that it was a non-issue. But they don't go around asking each other about their love lives, mostly because Devin's has been basically nonexistent since he met Hunter, and Hunter's has been predictable in its transience. "Er."

"Never mind, you don't have to tell me," Hunter says quickly, sounding a bit embarrassed.

"No, it's okay. I'm just trying to remember if it was Donald Howard or Robbie Williams from Take That that I had the bigger crush on."

"Oh wow, so you're a boy band gay?"

"Like you never jerked off to a New Kid on the Block," Devin scoffs.

Hunter makes a face. "Please. I definitely went through a Nick Lachey phase, though."

"I don't know who that is," Devin sniffs.

"Oh god, now I'm doubly embarrassed. 98 Degrees? He was married to Jessica Simpson?"

"I'm just kidding. I have an encyclopedic knowledge of 90s boy bands."

"Wow, you are cruel, messing with me like that."

Devin knocks his shoulder into Hunter's. "Someone has to keep you on your toes."

"That you do."

They share a smile, and Devin wonders what's going on in Hunter's head. He's usually so good at picking up on Hunter's moods, but this trip has turned all that upside down. He's learning about sides of Hunter he never expected to see. Hunter's been letting him in farther than Devin ever hoped to get. And every layer of Hunter that gets revealed only makes Devin love him more.

Wait. Hard stop. Love?

Devin's always been attracted to Hunter. He's liked him as a person, as a friend, admired his tenacity when it comes to their business, envied his casual bravery at literally facing death every day. But...love? Love means that when the day comes that Hunter meets someone he can stand for more than a week and gets remarried, or hell, when they get back to the desert and everything goes back to normal, that means Devin's heart is going to be well and truly broken.

It's not Hunter's fault. Devin wishes he could blame it on Hunter's perfect hair or his blinding smile or his sinfully sculpted forearms. But no, it's just who Hunter is that Devin has had the misfortune to fall in love with. There's nothing he can do about it, but he can try to salvage as much of his heart as he can. He backs away from Hunter, putting a few feet between them.

"Shall we go clean up for dinner? We're to attend the rehearsal for some reason, even though we're not being pressed into service at the wedding as far as I know."

"The rehearsal dinner is at the farm, so Gary said it's easier for us all to be there at the start," Hunter explains.

"There you go." Devin turns back toward the car. He nearly jumps out of his skin when he feels Hunter touch his elbow. "What?"

"Just, are you okay? I'm sorry if I laid too much of my baggage on you back there." His eyebrows are drawn close together and Devin's angry at himself for letting Hunter feel like he's done something wrong.

"No, all that was—I'm glad you told me, Hunter. Stop apologizing, okay? I'm your friend. Friends share this stuff, right?"

Hunter still doesn't look convinced, but he says, "Right."

They don't say much on the drive back to town.

TEN

THE BARN at Atkins Farm is only a barn in shape and size because the inside has been converted into an airy, well-lit space with a stage, a dance floor, and clusters of tables already partially decorated for tomorrow's wedding reception. Hunter and Devin arrive in time for the tail end of the rehearsal—the wedding ceremony itself will be in the small apple orchard behind the barn, with the reception in the barn and spilling over to the wide lawn outside, weather permitting.

Hunter's trying to regain his footing after his talk with Devin at the airfield that afternoon. He's been feeling off kilter since waking up in bed next to Devin that morning after the soundest sleep he'd had in years. Something about being in this place, away from the routine of SkyTrip, has him seeing Devin in a totally different way, and it's got him completely off balance.

At least Devin seems to be having a good time, and even if Hunter isn't used to having someone to talk to the way he'd opened up to Devin earlier, he can't deny that it was nice to have someone listen to him talk about his parents. Losing them is a hurt that has never completely healed over. But Devin had understood, had accepted Hunter's pain and was there for him. As usual.

This rehearsal dinner should have enough attendees where perhaps he and Devin can have some space from each other. This amount of non-work time they've spent together has given him funny ideas. He still hasn't been able to erase the vision of Devin in his swim trunks, and now he finds himself reflexively appreciating the fit of Devin's dark wash jeans and his tailored collared shirt, crisp white and reminding Hunter that Devin's got nice shoulders. And a tattoo. Yes, it's a nerdy tattoo, but it suits him. And this line of thought is completely not what Hunter needs right now.

"Rick! Hey, you need any help with Kai?" Hunter seizes his ex-brother-in-law's arm a bit manically.

"No, Anna's showing him off to some of the guests. You want a beer? There's an open bar."

"Yes, beer, good." He looks at Devin. "Want beer?"

Devin gives him an odd look. "Yes, me want beer. You get beer, bring back to cave."

Hunter's too keyed up to take offense at the joke. Or laugh at it. "I'll be right back."

The bar turns out to be rather crowded and Hunter spots a few familiar faces, including Zhen Lin, who went to college with Jillian and Hunter has met several times over the years. Jillian mentioned that she was flying in from her post in The New York Times's Shanghai bureau to be a bridesmaid.

"Hunter, how the hell are you?" Zhen asks in her brash, no-nonsense way.

"I'm good. You look sensational." He takes in her bright red party dress and matching crimson lipstick. Normally he'd flirt harder out of habit, but all he can think about is Devin and this strange new undercurrent to their interactions, which is clearly one-sided since Devin isn't acting any different. It's just Hunter making things weird.

"That's what being in love does to you." She points to a handsome, clean-shaven white guy in gray slacks and a cream linen shirt talking to Delphina. "That's my fiancé, Aidan Gorely. I fell in love with another journalist, of course."

"Congratulations." What's with everyone pairing off all of a sudden? He'd always thought Zhen was married to her work, and now she's marrying someone who does the same work she does. Huh.

"Thanks. So, Jillian tells me your new guy is a sweetheart. Things serious with you? Where is he, can I meet him?"

Hunter refrains from wincing, signals to the bartender for two beers to buy himself some time. "Devin, yeah, he's great. We're great. You can meet him. He's over there." He gestures vaguely and pulls his wallet out so he can tuck some cash into the tip jar.

Zhen laughs and shakes her head. "You are just the same, aren't you, Hunter?"

"What do you mean?"

"You know I had this nickname for you back when you and Jillian were dating. The Hedgehog."

Hunter frowns. "I don't get it."

"Prickly exterior but get inside and you're all fluff. Jillian got under your skin young, so she didn't see it. I hope your guy is tough enough to handle your sharp edges."

Hunter doesn't want to think about the implications of what she's saying. "I'm not drunk enough for these metaphors, Zhen."

"Me either. I'm getting a vodka tonic. I'll see you later?"

"Sure." Hunter beats a hasty retreat, locating Devin by the doors where he's talking to Gary. He thrusts a bottle at Devin, then downs half of his in two big gulps. Alcohol will make things better.

"You all right?" Devin hasn't taken a drink, just watches Hunter as if he thinks he might start a scene.

"I'm fine. Why is everyone worried about me all the time?"

Devin takes a step back at that and Hunter instantly feels like a dick.

"You know what, I'm just hungry."

"Dinner's a buffet," Gary supplies. "It's supposed to start any minute. Then you might want to get a couple more of those beers, because there's going to be toasts."

"Toasts?" Devin repeats. "As in speeches?"

"A lot of toasts," Gary says gravely. "Drink up, boys."

Gary wasn't wrong. By the third cousin singing the praises of Jillian and Aaron, Hunter strongly regrets not escaping with Devin when they had a chance. As it is, they're smiling and clapping at the appropriate places, but Hunter can tell Devin's as bored as he is. And despite the beer, he's not anywhere close to feeling the alcohol yet. He'd switch to something stronger, but he wants to be functional for the wedding tomorrow. Plus, there's nothing like the cliché of the ex getting smashed at the wedding of his former wife.

Eventually, the toasts end, the dessert—lemon meringue pie—is served. Someone hooks their phone up to the speaker system and starts blasting 70s funk. Aaron grabs Jillian and sweeps her onto the dance floor, dancing goofily. Hunter finds himself laughing as Aaron dips Jillian dangerously low. Jillian's giggling and looks about seventeen. He glances over at Devin, and he's smiling, too. He's got a dab of meringue on the corner of his mouth and without thinking about it, Hunter leans over and swipes it away with his thumb. It's barely a touch, but Devin jerks away from him like he's been burned. Hunter's stomach is doing that odd swooping thing again.

"Sorry. You had some meringue."

"Oh. Well, I'm a messy eater," Devin says quickly. "Worse than Kai, probably."

"You want to get out of here?" Hunter hears it come out of his mouth and hopes that Devin doesn't hear the implications in the phrase. Because that's not how Hunter meant it. Not at all.

"You want to go?" Devin looks surprised. "Seems like the party is just starting."

"Nah. Myrna's not going to let this go on much longer. She'll want us all to be fresh for tomorrow."

"Like Aaron's not going to go get drunk with his buddies right now?"

"I think Jillian's more likely to go out barhopping

than Aaron, but, yeah, I guess we should stay." Hunter can't explain why being alone with Devin seems like a really good idea, which is why it's probably a terrible one.

"Why don't we get one more drink, then head out?" Devin suggests as a compromise. "I'll get it."

"Okay." Hunter watches him walk away, then startles as Zhen suddenly takes Devin's seat and starts talking.

"I figured it out. You aren't so good at keeping secrets, are you, Hunter?"

ELEVEN

"WHAT?" Hunter honestly has no idea what she's talking about--unless she means the fact that he and Devin aren't actually together. Have they not been convincing? Hunter didn't think it would take much more than just being with each other all the time—there's no rule that couples must be affectionate in public. He supposes they could try, but then again, it might be too late for that.

"You and Devin. Come on, you can tell me." Zhen leans close; Hunter surmises she's had at least three of those vodka tonics. "Your secret is safe with me."

"So says the journalist," he returns.

"No, seriously, off the record. You guys are engaged, aren't you?"

"Huh?" Now she's completely lost him.

"You and Devin. I noticed how you look at each other, like you want to devour each other, but are holding back. It's because you don't want to steal Jillian's thunder, right? But you can tell me!" Zhen's practically salivating at the thought of a hot scoop.

"Tell you what?" Devin's back, two fresh bottles in his hands. He hands one to Hunter but doesn't sit.

"You guys are gonna get married," she sing-songs. "And live happily ever after. Maybe adopt a kid? No— two! Kids need siblings, Hunter," she declares firmly.

"You're drunk," Hunter says.

"And you're deflecting." She glances up at Devin. "You can tell me. I'm Zhen, by the way."

"Hi, Zhen."

"Zhen thinks we're secretly engaged and don't want Jillian to know." Hunter's voice holds all the apology he can muster.

Devin raises a single eyebrow. Hunter spares a moment to be impressed by that. "Does she now?"

"I'm engaged, too." Zhen thrusts her left hand in Hunter's face. He blinks and the giant diamond engagement ring on her fourth finger comes into focus.

"Jesus, Zhen, that thing looks like it could feed a small country for a year."

"Aidan's rich. Well, his parents are. What kind of ring did you get Devin?"

"Who says I didn't do the proposing?" Devin says with mock indignation. He drags an empty chair into the space between Hunter and Zhen, and Hunter has to admit he feels better with Devin as a buffer.

"Tell me how you did it! I love proposal stories." Zhen's begging now.

"Well...promise you won't tell anyone?" Devin says coyly.

"I promise." She mimes an exaggerated cross over her heart and leans in.

"Well, the first time I laid eyes on Hunter, the air smelt like coffee, that's a scent I've associated with him ever since. And he's rubbish at making coffee, so I'm always sure to bring him some decent stuff. So when I knew I wanted to spend the rest of my life with him, I decided to do it over coffee. I told him, Hunter, you're dearer to me than French roast, you're more addictive than cold brew, you're sweeter than a mochachino. Will you drink my coffee forever? Will you be my husband?"

Hunter's doing his best to keep a straight face, but he can't help his cheeks getting hot as Devin spins the lie out. He remembers that day in Starbucks, laying eyes on the cute Brit, falling into easy conversation with him, finding in him someone with an instant, unwavering belief that they could make something of Hunter's dream. Sometimes he thinks that belief saved his life for a second time. He wonders what Devin thought of him back then, before they became friends. What first impression did he give?

Zhen's practically drooling over the story, silly as it is. "And what did you say, Hunter?"

He balks at adding his own embroidery to the tale, but Devin nods at him encouragingly and winks, giving him enough confidence to answer. "Um. I said. Yes?"

Devin beams at him. "He said yes. And then he drank the cup of coffee I gave him and at the bottom was the ring."

Hunter snickers at that unlikely detail. Devin sticks his tongue out at him. Zhen's looking a little confused, so he clears his throat and adds, "Yeah, I, um, took it off because we didn't want to take away from Jillian's big day. You know."

"Wow, you two are so amazing." Zhen sighs. "And totally cute together. Come on, I want to see you lovebirds kiss."

Devin's smile drops as fast as a stone at 10,000 feet and Hunter's cheeks heat up again. "Come on, Zhen, we're not kissing so you can get your kicks watching two guys make out."

"You're no fun! Come on, just one little peck. Please? I'm going to be an old married lady soon; I'll need memories to sustain me."

Hunter looks at Devin helplessly. He shrugs in response. It's not a big deal, right? It'll at least sell the idea that they are a legitimate couple, once Zhen sobers up and realizes that ridiculous story could be nothing but a put on.

"You're a terrible person," Hunter says.

"I know. Now kiss!" Zhen pushes Devin's shoulder and suddenly there he is, right in front of Hunter. Devin's dear, familiar face wears a slightly stoic expression. Hunter wonders what his lips feel like, and then he realizes he can find out. All he has to do is—

Devin's mouth is on his before he can move. His lips are dry, and Hunter closes his eyes and moves his head so they slot more firmly together and avoid bumping noses. He opens his mouth just a fraction, deepening the kiss ever so slightly.

If you'd asked him yesterday what it would be like to kiss Devin Smith, he would have assumed it would be like kissing a friend. Not bad, but no spark. No fireworks. But kissing Devin feels like a Fourth of July spectacular, turning Hunter's skin hot, his stomach tight. His hands reach out to touch, grabbing the first part of Devin he can find, his thighs, sitting close together as they are. Devin tastes like the beer they've been drinking, and he smells vaguely spicy. Hunter's getting hard. It's when he registers that fact he jerks back, releasing his hold.

Devin's eyes are closed, and his mouth is still kiss-shaped. He looks like—he looks like he was doing a damn good job selling the kiss to Zhen, whose own mouth hangs open as if she got more than she bargained for.

"Wow," Zhen says. "I've got to find my fiancé immediately and get him to fuck me. See you tomorrow." Then she's up and across the room as if she's on an extremely tight deadline.

Neither of them speaks for a second, and then Devin says, "Well that was highly inappropriate."

The censure feels like a jab to his solar plexus. "I'm so sorry, Devin. I know you didn't sign up for that, and it was totally—"

"No, not you, her." Devin sits back in his chair. "You're fine. She's a maniac."

Hunter licks his lips, relief that Devin isn't angry at him making him giddy. "So that was just *fine*?"

Devin swivels his head quickly to look at him. "I've had worse," he says lightly and oh, Hunter really shouldn't push, but he can't seem to help himself.

"Have you had better, though?"

Devin puts a hand on his chin, as if pretending to

think. "I kissed a lip model once. He was pretty spectacular."

"There's no such thing as a lip model," Hunter argues, too happy that they're able to joke about this to feel slighted.

"There is too. He modeled for Carmex. Very sexy."

"Remind me to pick some up at the drugstore on the way home," Hunter grumbles. "Now can we get out of here?"

"Definitely."

TWELVE

AS DEVIN GETS ready for bed, he's got one thought looping around in his brain. He and Hunter kissed. He kissed Hunter Pike. Hunter Pike kissed him. And despite what he told Hunter, it had been the best kiss of his thirty-two years to date. By far. Not because the technique was out of this world or the moment magical. Honestly, Devin knows he can do better, and it wasn't exactly romantic to be blackmailed into a kiss by a perfect stranger. But that kiss tops Devin's list with a bullet because it was *Hunter*.

Whatever distance Devin has been trying to put between them isn't working because his feelings are only getting more difficult to ignore, let alone hide. And now he's about to go out there and sleep in the same bed as Hunter knowing what it feels like to kiss his bloody perfect lips and taste his bloody perfect mouth.

How exactly is he supposed to survive that?

He goes back into the bedroom, teeth clean, sleep clothes on. Hunter's sitting on his side of the bed with his phone in his hand, but he isn't looking at it. He's staring into space. Devin would give his entire Monty Python DVD collection to know what Hunter's thinking right now. Is he thinking about the kiss? Is he equally consumed with awkwardness, or has he already forgotten about it?

Devin tosses his dirty clothes on top of his suitcase and tries to think of anything to say that would sound normal in this situation. This situation is so far from normal he literally can't think of a thing.

"Er."

Hunter looks up.

Good start, Devin. "Do you think there's an iron I could use? Wouldn't do to be all wrinkly for the wedding."

Hunter hums. "I'm sure there is. I'll ask Myrna in the morning."

"Thanks. No rush. Not like I need to iron right now. It's late. Sort of. Well."

Hunter doesn't respond, and he doesn't move. Devin hadn't minded getting into the bed last night when his friend was already burrowed under the covers, but with the light still on and Hunter right there, he feels extraordinarily self-conscious about slipping into their—*the* bed. It's not theirs. It's just a bed. That they happen to be sharing. Because why again? Oh yes, because Hunter is emotionally incompetent and Devin's the poor sod who loves him.

That mental pep talk gives Devin enough gumption to go over to the damn bed already. As he approaches, Hunter stands up.

"I better brush my teeth."

"Yes." They look at each other for a moment. It's impossible not to wish that Hunter's brushing his teeth so when he kisses Devin again he'll be minty fresh. But that's not happening, maybe ever again.

When Hunter finally moves toward the bathroom, Devin turns off the light on his side and climbs into bed, pulling the summer-weight comforter over his chest. He tries not to listen to the sounds of Hunter running water in the sink, of something clattering on the countertop. All those little domestic noises you hear when you live with someone. When you're intimate with them.

This little game of theirs is really fucking with Devin's brain. He tries doing the times tables backwards in his head to empty his mind of anything but numbers. Numbers make sense. Numbers don't tell people you're dating when you are doing nothing of the sort. Numbers don't kiss you and leave you breathless and aching for more. He's at six times seven equals forty-two and Hunter hasn't come to bed yet when he falls asleep.

A NOISE WAKES Devin some undetermined time later, but it's still pitch black in Jillian's parents' guest room, so it must be the middle of the night. But what noise? He listens, and it comes again, a low, anguished moan. Through the fog of sleep, he realizes it's Hunter, tossing and groaning. Devin pushes the covers away, touches Hunter on the shoulder. He doesn't wake up.

"Hunter," Devin whispers.

Hunter lets out a whimper that sets Devin's sympathetic nerves into overdrive. His heart's beating fast as he shakes Hunter again, a little harder. "Hunter. Wake up."

Hunter's head twists again, side to side on the pillow, and he lets out a single word. "Stop!"

Devin knows the nightmare has Hunter deep in its clutches and he doesn't know what to do about it. He's breathing as fast as Hunter, trying to figure out the best course of action. He decides to try shaking him again one more time, when Hunter's eyes fly open, and he goes rigid. Devin can't know if Hunter's still in the nightmare or not, so he starts babbling. "Hunter, you're okay, you're with me, we're in Apple Vale, for the wedding, remember?"

"Devin?" Hunter's voice is hoarse, but he sounds lucid enough.

Devin sags with relief. "Yeah, Devin." He twists around to grab a bottle of water from the nightstand and hands it to Hunter. "You had a nightmare."

Hunter scoots up the bed and takes the water. He has trouble unscrewing the cap, so Devin takes it back from him, opens the bottle himself, then passes it back. Hunter takes a shaky sip.

"You okay now?" Devin asks.

Hunter's face is stone. "I'm okay," he croaks. "It was —it was a bad one. Haven't had one like that in a while."

"I'm sorry." Devin isn't exactly surprised that he's experiencing some side effects after what he shared today. He knows that Hunter's time in the military left him with invisible scars. Plus, everything being here for the wedding might be stirring up. Hunter's dealing with a lot right now. Devin can't help feeling guilty about letting his nose get out of joint because of one awkward kiss. He sighs. He might regret it later, but he can't help wanting to be there for Hunter, in whatever way Hunter needs that to be.

"It's okay," Hunter says, passing the water back to Devin. "It was—better. With you waking me up. With you here."

"That's good." He feels a soft swell of pride at being able to help Hunter. "You want to talk about it?"

"Not really. Just—stay here?"

He says it like he's not sure Devin will. Which is ridiculous. As if Devin would willingly leave Hunter when it's clear he's needed. He sets the water bottle back on the nightstand, settles back onto his pillow. He turns on his side to face Hunter's profile. Even in the dark he can make out the strong, proud nose, the suggestion of his lips. Devin can conjure up the feel of them now. He knows what Hunter's breath tastes like. He almost wishes he didn't.

"Do you think you'll be able to go back to sleep?" Devin keeps his voice low in case Hunter's already managed to drop off.

But Hunter answers, voice just as quiet. The dark makes it a million times more intimate. "I think so. In a minute."

"I do times tables."

"Excuse me?"

"In my head, when I want to fall asleep. Times tables. Backward. Does the trick every time."

"I doubt I could even do them forward," Hunter says.

"Then you could think about, I don't know, naming engine parts in a Cessna Twin Otter."

Hunter's chuckle is soft, but it soothes the tight knot that Devin didn't realize he'd formed in his chest. "I'll give it a shot."

"Do that."

They fall silent, and Devin counts Hunter's breaths until he's drowsy again, the adrenaline fading. Then Hunter shifts, and his arm brushes against Devin's. Stays there. He doesn't know if Hunter's asleep or awake, but he doesn't move his arm and Devin falls asleep with the reassuring, terrifying weight of Hunter at his side.

THIRTEEN

HUNTER WAKES UP BEFORE DEVIN, just as he had the morning before, though it's slightly later than yesterday. He's always been pretty good at judging the time. He estimates it's a few minutes before seven. He slept hard and deep after waking up from the nightmare. After Devin had practically rescued him from it.

He's used to the nightmares, sort of. They started after his parents died, went away when he was on active duty, then started up again around the time he was discharged and the divorce was going through. Since establishing SkyTrip, they've tapered off, but always leave him feeling disoriented, vaguely ill. He doesn't think about them too hard, when he's awake, but they're usually a variation on a theme: the people he loves are in trouble and he can't get to them in time. At first, it was, predictably, his parents. Later, his team members, fellow soldiers in a war most people didn't know they were fighting. Jillian featured in them from time to time. But last night it was Devin who was inexplicably in the grip of some unspeakable evil, Devin who was going to die if Hunter wasn't fast enough, smart enough, brave enough to save him.

But Devin had saved him first.

Now he's sleeping, head tipped toward Hunter so Hunter can see his fair lashes brushing his cheekbones. He's got a few freckles on his nose, a few lines around his eyes that weren't there when Hunter met him. They're both getting older.

A thought, unbidden, comes into his head. *What are we waiting for?* He thinks about last night, not the nightmare part, which was bad, but then good, Devin warm and alive and comforting Hunter as if it was his job. But before, when they'd been talking and bantering and drinking together at the party. It had been...different between them, Hunter thinks. He came here thinking he needed a shield from Jillian and everything she represents, but he's barely thought about her at all. He's mostly just happy she's getting the life she deserves, and that he's around to see it. He doesn't want her back. But he's beginning to realize that maybe there is something else he does want.

He thinks about the kiss. About how inexplicably good it was. He looks at Devin's lips, framed by his neat, silky soft beard, mere inches away, and realizes he wants to do it again.

He wants to do it when it's not a performance.

But then he remembers and his stomach plummets faster than 9.8 meters per second per second. This entire weekend has been a performance. Devin's not really his boyfriend, he's just the world's nicest friend-slash-business partner. And yeah, he hadn't seemed repulsed by kissing Hunter, but it wasn't as if they'd had much of a choice. In three years, Devin has never once hinted that he wants their relationship to be anything different from what it is. This whole stupid date thing was Hunter's idea from the start. Devin is just a really, really good friend, and Hunter doesn't have a right to ask him to consider anything else. He's still broken, after all. The evidence is right there, in the nightmare that ripped into him last night, that woke Devin up and forced him to play nursemaid.

It doesn't matter how much he wants to kiss Devin. It's not going to happen again. And if it wouldn't add too much drama to a day that's supposed to be all about Jillian's future, he'd march downstairs and come clean right this minute.

He eases out of bed, grabs his running shoes. He's not letting one stupid kiss mess up his friendship with Devin. Devin deserves so much better than Hunter Pike.

HUNTER'S apparently already up and gone by the time Devin makes his way downstairs, yawning and desperate for coffee. Myrna tells him that Hunter grabbed his own caffeine and then headed out for a run before the humidity sets in.

"We're off to the hairdressers in a few. Help yourself to what's in the fridge and we'll see you at the ceremony later. Oh, and Devin—there's an iron in the laundry room. Just past the pantry." Myrna points down the hall.

"Okay," Devin says, brain still muddled as he pours himself a cup of coffee. Then he remembers his throw-away comment about his wrinkly suit last night. Hunter must have said something to her. "Oh, right, iron, check. Thanks."

She just laughs and pats his shoulder on her way out of the kitchen. Devin's contemplating taking a swim before Hunter gets back when someone else enters the room.

"Devin!" It's Jillian, casual in jeans and a tank top that shows off slim but toned arms.

"Morning." He hesitates. They've never been alone together, and he can't think of anything to say. "Er—if you're looking for Hunter, I think he went for a run."

She smiles at him brightly. "Actually, I'm glad for a moment alone with you. This weekend has been such a whirlwind—so many people, my face hurts from all the smiling."

"If weddings are anything, it isn't relaxing," Devin agrees, having been to his share of family nuptials.

"Exactly. Aaron and I are desperately going to need our honeymoon after this."

Devin chuckles lightly. "That's what my parents always say."

Jillian's smile turns quizzical for a moment, but she doesn't ask for clarification. Instead, she leans across the bar and lowers her voice. "I have to thank you for getting Hunter to come this weekend. I know he didn't really want to, and I'm sure you're the reason he got on the plane."

"Oh. Er. Not really. I mean, he asked me to come," Devin says. That much at least, is true.

"And he wouldn't have if you hadn't said yes. So, thank you. Maybe you think it's horrible of me to want him here—but Hunter and me, we're not like most ex-married people. We've always been better friends than lovers, anyway."

Devin resists cringing at the word lovers. What is happening right now? When did he and Jillian become BFFs?

"Anyway, it's so important to me that he's here. It's important to my folks, too. They've always considered him another son, even before his parents died. And I know he loves them, but he'll deny himself things he loves because he doesn't think he deserves them—well, I don't have to tell you, I'm sure you know."

Devin's about to protest, but on second thought he does know what Jillian means. Hunter always pushes himself twice as far as anyone else, is twice as hard on himself. It would be like him to deny himself the pleasure of being around people who care about him.

But in the end, he hadn't. He asked Devin for help, and it warms Devin's pathetic, Hunter-obsessed heart that he's been able to do this for his friend. Jillian knows Hunter better than anyone else. Maybe she can help him figure out how to stop himself from falling even harder for someone he can't ever have. Of course, that would mean telling her the truth.

It's not Devin's truth to share.

He clears his throat, tries to put some of what he's feeling into words without giving the game away. "I don't know exactly what Hunter told you, but this thing between us is still rather...new. How do I—I mean, I haven't told him exactly how much I—and I don't know if he—" Devin breaks off, sighs. This is a bad idea. Even if Devin knew what he wanted to ask, Jillian's the last person he should come to for advice.

But she just smiles, unfazed by Devin's words, or lack thereof. "Devin, I get it. Hunter's amazing, but he's not the most self-aware guy in the world. I guess that's why I was a little surprised when he told me he was bringing you to the wedding."

She reaches out, puts a soft, strong hand on Devin's arm. He appreciates the anchor because her words are setting him adrift. "He talked about you nonstop for three years, but he never seemed to hear himself gush, because he was always going on those pointless internet dates. But then he told me you were his date to the wedding, and I thought he finally figured out how he felt. I also know, having been in your shoes, that sometimes it's hard for him to transition from friend to boyfriend. I practically had to blackmail him to get him to kiss me for the first time."

Devin thinks back to Zhen. "I can relate."

"Hunter may not be the sharpest knife in the drawer when it comes to emotions, but he's the sweetest guy in the world when he's in love. And the way he looks at you —I know what Hunter Pike looks like when he's in love. And he's in love with you, Devin Smith. You just have to give him a little time to realize it."

Jillian glances over Devin's shoulder to the clock on the wall and winces. "Oh, man, I have to go. Hair and makeup and all that stuff. But I will see you later!" She leans over the bar, smacks a quick kiss to Devin's cheek, and then she's gone, as if she drops bombs about people being in love with other people all the time.

Devin puts a hand to his cheek where she kissed him and rubs absently. He looks down at his empty mug of coffee. Was that a dream? Is he still asleep? He could have sworn Jillian had just said words to the effect that Hunter Pike is in love with him. Which is impossible. And ridiculous. And impossible. Wait—he already said that. To himself. His internal monologue is skipping like one of his gran's 45s.

But what if it isn't impossible? What if there is a chance? He allows himself a total of ten glorious, awful seconds to imagine what it would be like to be loved by Hunter, totally and completely. To have him as a friend and a business partner and, yes, a lover, too. To feel Hunter's lips against his again, to feel the strength of his body straining toward Devin's, to touch him and kiss him and bring him pleasure. To make Hunter laugh. To be there for him when he cries.

Distantly, Devin hears the front door open and shut. He blinks away the vision of being with Hunter before he tortures himself any further. And then Hunter himself walks in, face red and sweaty, out of breath from his run. Devin can smell him, masculine and salty, from across the room. His mouth fills with saliva, his body tightening in response to Hunter's mere presence. Abruptly, he turns away, pretends to be busy pouring himself the dregs of the pot of coffee.

"Any chance of a cup for me?" Hunter asks.

"I'll make another pot." Devin's shocked that his voice comes out sounding relatively normal.

"You're the best," Hunter says. "I'm going to take a shower."

Devin hums. He does not imagine joining Hunter in said shower but concentrates very hard on refilling the water reservoir on the coffee machine. He hears Hunter start to leave, but then—

"Oh! Did Myrna tell you where to find the iron?"

"Yep."

"Good. Okay."

"Okay."

"Well, I'm going to go shower."

"So you said."

"Right. Thanks for the coffee."

"No problem."

Hunter finally leaves; Devin hears his steps as he jogs up the stairs to their room. He sags against the countertop. What the hell is he going to do?

FOURTEEN

THE WEDDING IS SET for late afternoon. Hunter's only job is to show up and look happy. He stares at his reflection in the guest room bathroom mirror and tries on a smile. Disaster. He looks manic and fake and he doesn't know why this is so hard and Devin is supposed to make it easier and he's been weird all day and Hunter's not sure if he can do this and—

"Hunter? You all right in there?"

Devin's voice on the other side of the door; Hunter almost sags with relief. They'd sort of missed each other all day—Devin had gone out to run an errand in the car just as Hunter came back from his post-run shower, then didn't return until it was time to start getting ready. He took his suit down the laundry room to de-wrinkle it, and Hunter has been in the bathroom donning his old black suit and trying to get his shit together. And failing, obviously.

"I can't tie my tie," he says. He's too far gone to worry about seeming helpless.

There's a silence. Then, "Can I come in?"

In answer, Hunter twists the knob. Devin stands on the other side, and he looks—Hunter takes a moment to find the word he wants—*resplendent*. His suit is charcoal gray and made of some soft material in what seems like a perfect weight for a midsummer's evening wedding. His white shirt is crisp and clean underneath, and he's got a matching gray waistcoat to pull the whole thing together. His tie is dark blue, identical in color to the little pocket square on his left breast. His hair and beard are neatly combed. Hunter's gaze falls on Devin's black dress shoes.

"No sneakers?"

"I left my dressy ones at home. Now, what's this about your tie?"

Hunter backs up to let Devin into the small space and holds up a strip of black fabric. It's wider than Devin's, probably horribly out of fashion. "It's been a while since I had to wear one of these," he says weakly, as Devin surveys his outfit wide-eyed.

"Apparently. You said your suit was older than your wedding to Jillian, but I didn't think you meant truly vintage."

Hunter swallows, closes his eyes. "It was my dad's. We were about the same size. I wore it to his funeral." Why hadn't he taken the time to buy something new? Devin looks like he stepped off the pages of *British GQ* and Hunter's going to look like a kid wearing his father's suit to the school dance.

Devin doesn't say anything, and Hunter opens his eyes. Devin's mouth is a hard line. He's either trying not to laugh or trying not to cry. Hunter's not sure which would be more humiliating. He starts to push past, to forget about the tie and just go, but Devin puts a hand on his arm. "Wait. We can work with this. Just give me a second."

Hunter stops. He lets Devin tug him out of the jacket.

"It's a new shirt, at least," Devin mutters. He puts a hand on his chin like a sartorial schoolmaster. "Stay here." He disappears and returns after a moment with a different tie. "Here's what we're going to do. It's warm enough that you can take the jacket off almost right away. Your shirt fits you well, and this tie will update the whole thing. It's one of mine. Give it a go." When Hunter just stares at him, Devin sighs and sets to work tying the tie around Hunter's neck himself. He mutters a few things under his breath. Hunter's too grateful to worry if Devin's exasperated with him.

Devin works efficiently, and Hunter enjoys watching him while his attention is on the tie. He smells good, too, like laundry starch and beard oil. Hunter sways a little closer trying to pick out the individual scents—almond, maybe? Or vanilla?

"Er, now the trousers," Devin says, a funny catch in his voice.

Hunter forces himself to lean away from Devin, realizing he's lost all notion of personal space.

"What about the trousers?"

"They're much too bulky. You ought to have them tailored. Not much we can do about that now, but I can at least—" Devin reaches for Hunter's belt and Hunter finds himself wishing Devin was doing that under different circumstances. He wrenches his mind away from that forbidden thought and lets Devin adjust the waistline of the pants by doing something with an inner button Hunter had never noticed and by tightening his belt. Once everything's fastened again Devin says, "Not bad. You'll do."

He moves out of the way so Hunter can inspect himself in the mirror. He looks respectable, maybe not as stylish or elegant as Devin, but the slim dark green tie goes nicely with his eyes, his white dress shirt is fine, and his black trousers somehow look more fitted. He'll have to wear the jacket for the ceremony, but Devin's right, he can take it off for the reception and not feel like a dowdy cousin.

"Thanks, Devin. You're a miracle worker."

"I've just watched a lot of *Queer Eye*," Devin says with a wave of his hand, making Hunter smile, and not a desperate grimace but the genuine article. However modest Devin is being, Hunter knows that he owes the success of the weekend to his friend.

"Seriously, Dev, what would I do without you?"

"Let's hope we'll never have to find out," Devin says lightly. "Now, we better go. The ceremony's not going to wait for us."

Devin drives, naturally. They don't talk on the way. Hunter's brain is all muddled. It's not fair of Devin to be so put together—figuratively and literally. It makes Hunter extra aware of just what a bad bargain he is—a divorced veteran with a touch of PTSD who jumps out of airplanes for a living. Leaving out the fact he lives in a tiny trailer and his usual mode of transportation is a motorcycle since his truck is so temperamental, what on earth could he possibly offer a partner? He snorts. No wonder he had to force someone to pretend to love him for a weekend.

"What's so funny over there?" Devin asks as they slip into the Atkins Farm parking lot. It's already full, and a glance at the dash clock shows they'll need to hustle to make it on time.

"I'll tell you later," Hunter says. "Let's go watch my ex-wife get hitched."

THE WEDDING IS, in a word, lovely. Jillian is lovely in her off-white floor-length lace dress with a crown of white roses making her look young and carefree. Aaron is lovely in a light gray summer suit with a white rose in his lapel. The music is lovely, the ceremony is just the right length—not too long, not too short. Everything is lovely.

And Devin couldn't care less.

He only cares about Hunter, about how he's smiling with his mouth but not his eyes. How his shoulders round over when he thinks no one is looking. But Devin sees everything. He's starting to realize that even though Jillian loves Hunter so much she wants him to be at her wedding to another person, her entire family considers Hunter family, too, and Devin's head over heels for the guy, the truth is, Hunter Pike has a pretty poor opinion of himself.

Devin remembers what Jillian said—that Hunter denies himself things because he doesn't think he deserves them—and his hands form fists of their own accord. To hell with that. Hunter deserves the world, and he's not afraid to fight anybody who thinks otherwise— even if he ends up fighting Hunter himself.

They manage to make it through the thunderous applause at the end of the ceremony, then the reception line, plus the champagne toast that kicks off the reception, Hunter wearing his fake, pasted-on smile the entire time. Devin is finally able to drag him to the side for a moment of privacy as the guests migrate to the barn for the buffet dinner and dancing.

"Are you all right?" he demands.

Hunter blinks at him. "Of course. Do I not seem all right?"

"You seem like a bloody automaton. Now, either tell me what's wrong or we're duct taping out of here."

Hunter drops the smile and Devin sighs with relief. "We can't go yet. Jillian will be crushed."

"Jillian is surrounded by a hundred other people; she won't notice if we leave."

"No, no, I'm fine." Hunter straightens his shoulders as if going into battle.

"All right, then let's make you more comfortable at least." Devin tugs on Hunter's hideous jacket and helps him slip it off. He drapes it over the back of a chair. "With any luck someone will spill lighter fluid on this, and it will not come home with us."

"But that's my d—" Hunter stops himself. He shrugs. "You're probably right."

Devin touches Hunter's arm to soften what he's about to say. "Hunter, it's the sweetest, saddest thing I've ever heard that you wore your father's suit to his funeral, but it's time to let it go, don't you think?"

He holds Hunter's gaze until Hunter nods. He even shows a tiny sliver of a smile. It gives Devin hope.

"Good. Now, we're going to take way too much food from the buffet—I hear there's shrimp—and we're going to order a lot of drinks and we're going to have fun even if it kills us. All right?"

"All right. But let's skip the shrimp. Shellfish at a buffet is never a good idea."

"Noted. See, you've saved me from a night heaving my guts out. What would I do without you?" Devin hopes that in the walk to the buffet Hunter won't examine his wording too closely.

He doesn't expect what Hunter says next. "Let's hope we never find out."

FIFTEEN

"AND THEN, she blew chunks all over her future father-in-law's shoes. It was both disgusting and the most supreme example of poetic justice I've ever had the good fortune to witness." Devin's finale to one of their most epic SkyTrip customer stories has everyone at the table doubled over with laughter, Hunter included. He was on hand for the event, but no one tells a story like Devin, full of witty asides and borderline-catty judgements. He wipes tears from his eyes as he takes the final sip of his beer. Devin's glass is empty as well. He pushes back from the table, leans close to Devin's ear so he can be heard over the eighties cover band.

"I'm going to get us another round."

Devin turns his head and suddenly they're only a few inches apart. If Hunter leaned down, they could be...no, that's the absolute wrong direction his thoughts should be headed. It's the dozenth time he's had to remind himself that he and Devin might be here together, but they're not together, together. After a few pints of strong local microbrew, Hunter's having a slight bit of trouble remembering why that is. Every time he catches sight of Devin's kind eyes, his laughing mouth, he remembers the unfailing support he's given him since they got in the car to go to the airport three days ago and Hunter just wants—more.

Still, kissing Devin is not allowed.

He picks his way between half empty tables and folding chairs littered with jackets and purses to get the bar. Most everyone's on the dance floor. The wedding has been a complete success. Jillian's radiant with joy, Aaron twinkles with happiness every time his gaze lands on his bride. And why shouldn't they be happy? They just declared in front of everyone they love that they want to belong to each other for the rest of their lives. Tonight, they're going to the nicest hotel in Apple Vale and tomorrow morning getting on a plane to Costa Rica for a week-long honeymoon.

Sex vacation, more likely. Hunter snorts internally. If he had a week in Costa Rica with Devin, they'd never make it out of their room. Well, Devin would probably want to go explore the beaches and the rainforest. Zip lining would be fun if he could talk Devin into it. Then they could find a little private beach somewhere, go skinny dipping, and....

He stops in front of the bar and rubs his temples. He must have drunk more than he thought if he's imagining going on a sex vacation with Devin. He shakes the notion out of his head and orders a beer for Devin and a water for himself.

While he's waiting, he scans the party. Gary and Myrna are talking with Aaron's mother and some of his other relatives. Zhen and Aidan are slow dancing, even though the band is in the middle of "Love Shack." Aaron and Jillian are by the cake table, talking to some Doctors-Without-Borders-types. He spots Rick with little Kai asleep on his shoulder. He wonders if Devin's ever thought about having kids. He'd probably be a good dad.

And there he goes, not able to keep his mind off Devin for more than a minute. His gaze swings back to their table, where he'd left Devin holding court with a group of Jillian's friends from the hospital. They've mostly dispersed, but he sees someone sit down in his spot, a youngish guy with dark hair and an easy smile. He's saying something and Devin's—Devin's *laughing*. The other guy laughs, too, and scoots his chair an inch closer. Hunter knows flirting when he sees it, and this guy is flirting with Hunter's wedding date. Not okay.

"Your drinks." The bartender taps Hunter on the shoulder, and he turns, surprised. He stuffs a bill into the tip jar without looking at the denomination and grabs the two glasses. He gets back to the table just in time to hear the newcomer ask Devin if he wants to dance.

"Oh, well." There's hesitation in Devin's voice, but Hunter's not sure why. Is it because he doesn't want to dance, or because he's supposed to be here as Hunter's date and dancing with someone else would be weird, or—"Hunter, you're back."

Hunter offers something like a smile to the pair. "I'm back," he echoes. "Here you go." He hands Devin his beer and locks eyes with the new guy.

"Hunter, this is Sean."

"Hi, Sean."

Sean smiles and tosses off a little half wave. "Hi there. Devin and I were going to hit the dance floor."

"Were you?" Hunter doesn't blink and Sean's smile grows a tad uncertain.

"You know what, I think I'm going to sit this one out. Nice to meet you, Sean," Devin says neutrally.

Sean looks between them for a moment as if debating saying something else—he even opens his mouth, but Hunter narrows his eyes at him and he simply gets up from the table and backs away, melting into the crowd on the dance floor.

Hunter slides into the spot Sean vacated and takes a sip of his water. "What did I miss?"

"Nothing, just someone attempting to be friendly," Devin says. He's got a little groove between his eyebrows. Hunter hates that he's the one who's put it there. Suddenly, he feels tired. He's being spectacularly unfair to Devin.

"I'm sorry, I shouldn't have interrupted," he says quickly. "You should go find him. Go dance."

"What?" Now the groove is deeper.

"I mean, I could see he liked you and I got—I'm sorry. You should be able to—"

"You got what, Hunter?"

Hunter stares at his glass instead of at Devin. He makes himself say the word. "Jealous, I guess?"

"I'm not going to make you look bad, if that's what you're thinking," Devin says quietly.

He looks up at that. "Jesus, that's not it at all, Devin. I'm just saying, this has been a fun night after all. I guess I thought we were having fun together. But you deserve—"

"Don't tell me what I deserve, Hunter Pike." Devin's voice is almost a growl. "And we were having fun together. You and me. And if I want to dance with somebody, I'll bloody well dance with them."

Hunter takes a beat to make sure he's finished before letting out a surprised but firm, "Okay."

Devin looks somewhat taken aback by Hunter's agreement. But he nods. "Good. So." He pauses and takes a breath. "Do you want to dance?"

"Me? You want to dance with me?" Hunter's not sure why his voice is coming out all squeaky, but he doesn't think on it too long because Devin's nodding and standing up and offering Hunter a hand.

"All right," he says, putting his hand into Devin's outstretched one. Devin doesn't let go until they reach the dance floor. Hunter's collar feels hot, and he feels like everyone is looking at them, only they aren't. The band's gone from "Love Shack" to "Like a Virgin" which isn't as easy to dance to, but at least it's not a slow song. If he has any more contact with Devin's suit-clad body, he might catch on fire.

As it is, they laughingly fall into a rhythm around each other, not touching, but near enough. Devin's a natural, of course, shimmying and swaying and singing along to the chorus, making Hunter laugh and not feel so self-conscious about his own movements. It's not that he doesn't like dancing. But it's been a very long time.

One song turns into three. Zhen and Aidan wander over, joining them in shouting out the words to "Girls Just Wanna Have Fun." Jillian and Aaron show up midway through the song, though they get called away almost immediately to say goodbye to departing guests.

Then it happens. The band switches gears and Cindy Lauper gives way to George Michael. The strains of "Careless Whisper" fill the space. Zhen clings to Aidan like a baby sloth to his much taller one.

Hunter slows down, realizes how sweaty he's gotten, and makes a show of rolling up his sleeves, buying himself some time. Devin's sleeves are already rolled up, revealing his surprisingly muscular forearms, slender though they may be. They exchange a glance and Hunter's about to stuff down his inappropriate inclinations and just dance with his friend for god's sake, but Devin says, "Want to get some air?"

He nods and follows Devin outside. He's surprisingly disappointed at not getting to experience the feeling of Devin in his arms.

SIXTEEN

AFTER THE SWEATY heat of the dance floor, the balmy midsummer night air feels good on Devin's skin. He'd removed his jacket and waistcoat earlier in the night, and now he loosens his tie and undoes the first couple of buttons on his shirt. He doesn't have a particular destination in mind, so he walks past the people clumped outside, a couple of them smoking, a few talking quietly under lanterns. The carpark is on one side, the rolling fields of the old farm on the other. Devin heads into the dark, toward the smell of freshly mown grass. He can feel Hunter following and he doesn't know what to make of it.

Hunter's been at his side the entire night, except for when he went to get drinks and came back only to be rather endearingly jealous over some random bloke who only wanted a dance. He's been endearing all night, in fact. And Devin's confused over how much of their laughter and quips and the jealousy and the dancing is because they are two friends pretending to be in love or if —if there's something between them. Something that's not all on Devin's side. If Hunter feels—Jillian said love, but Devin's not going to get ahead of himself—if Hunter feels something besides friendship.... His hands go sweaty at the very thought of it.

"Devin, wait up." Hunter's a few feet behind now. Devin slows, and Hunter trots up to him, falling into step beside. They're following a gravel road up a gentle rise. Devin doesn't know what they'll find at the top, but he has to keep moving or he'll do something he might regret.

"Are you okay?" Hunter asks. "Did I do something wrong?"

"No, of course not." It's not Hunter's fault he's twitchy with want. "I'm just—it was getting claustrophobic in there."

They've reached the top of the rise. Devin stops and turns around. The lights of the party seem far away at the bottom of the hill. They could be miles away. All he can hear are crickets and his own breathing. And Hunter, his feet crunching on the gravel road.

"There's the Big Dipper," Hunter says.

Devin allows himself to glance over. He can make Hunter out in the dark, his white shirt glowing in what little light there is. His head is tipped back as he looks at the sky. Devin does the same, spotting the constellation easily. "The stars are brighter at home."

"You're right," Hunter says. He sounds a little surprised.

"I'm—" Devin stops. He was about to turn it into a

joke. How he's always right. But he doesn't feel particularly right at the moment. He feels itchy and nervous and Hunter's right there, and he doesn't know what's real and what's this stupid wedding date business. Maybe he doesn't care anymore. The beer and the dancing and the fact that Hunter's here with him instead of literally anyplace else on earth makes him feel a bit reckless.

Hunter doesn't let him off the hook. "You're?"

"I'm—look, a shooting star." The line of light streaks across the sky above them and is gone.

"I saw it," Hunter says, a bit of wonder in his voice.

"Did you make a wish?"

"No."

"Well go on then." Devin nudges Hunter's side. He hadn't realized Hunter was standing so close.

"Did you?"

"Of course."

Devin looks at Hunter's face, watches him close his eyes. He moves his mouth a little, like a little kid, as he makes his wish. It makes Devin smile.

Hunter's eyes fly open. "What?"

"What, what?"

"Why are you smiling?"

"Because you're adorable, Hunter Pike." Devin almost claps his hand over his mouth. Shit. He's got to be more careful.

"No, I'm not. I'm grumpy and insecure and I work too much and I'm hard to get along with."

"Oh, you're just fishing for compliments now, aren't you?"

"No—well. No." Hunter laughs a little. "I'm glad you think I'm adorable," he says quietly.

"You are?"

"I think you're sort of adorable, too, you know."

Now Devin knows he's dreaming. "Really?"

"I think—" Hunter grabs Devin's hand and presses it gently. "Jesus, Devin, I've wanted to kiss you all night."

Devin's heart feels like it's going to hammer through his rib cage. "You did? Why haven't you then?" Stupid thing to ask, but he's buying time before they go to a place they can't get back from.

"Because I didn't want to do it as a performance for all those people."

Devin swallows. Hunter's still holding his hand. He raises his free hand and puts it on Hunter's waist. Nothing ventured, nothing gained and all that.

"There's no one else around now," he says, low and meaningful.

Hunter's reply is to put his other hand on the small of Devin's back, drawing him close. They're of similar height, Devin edging Hunter out by an inch or two. He only has to tilt his head slightly to make their mouths meet. They kiss slow and unrushed, learning each other's shape. It's far different from the first time, which was self-consciously fast and over-compensatory. That was for Zhen. This is just for them, their only audience the earth under their feet and the stars above.

Hunter tastes good—a little sour, like the beer they've been drinking all night, but beneath that, there's a seductive earthiness. Devin chases the flavor with his tongue, and Hunter opens up to him, sweet at first, then some invisible line is crossed because he's kissing back harder now, chasing something of his own. And it feels so good—so *fucking* good—to hold Hunter and to kiss him that Devin feels a little sick with it.

How is it this good, after all the years he spent trying not to imagine what Hunter kissed like, for fear of damaging their improbable, vital friendship? How long has Hunter wanted this and how long will he want it? For how much longer can Devin call him his? If it's only for this moment, with their lips locked and their breath one and the same, he doesn't care. Hunter could be his for merely a single second, and he'd still want this. He wants Hunter for a lifetime, but that's okay. That doesn't matter. Hunter wants him right now, and that's enough.

It will have to be enough.

They sink to the grass, and Hunter's unbuttoning the rest of Devin's buttons and Devin's untying the knot he put in Hunter's tie himself hours ago. For a while it all feels so incredible Devin can't think, and he revels in the not-thinking, the not-worrying, the-not caring about anything that might happen tomorrow. It's all Hunter, around him, above him, as they stroke hands over stomachs and across chests, as they kiss down the sides of necks and tongue the hollows of throats.

Devin dips his fingers in the hair at the base of Hunter's skull, so long and soft, so eminently tuggable. He tries it and Hunter groans—moans, really—so he does it again and the sound Hunter makes has Devin's cock hardening painfully fast.

From there it's easy as anything to unbuckle, unbutton, unzip. It's fast, it's messy and a little dangerous right out there in the open, where anyone might see them, but Devin relishes the danger. Hunter drops himself out of airplanes three times a day—how could sex with Devin on a hillside in upstate New York even rate?

The word sticks in Devin's brain. Sex. Sex with Hunter. Jesus. Then they've got their hands on each other's cocks and Hunter's feels thick and hot against Devin's palm. Hunter's hand is rough and just the right amount of pressure on Devin's prick. They don't stop kissing as they bring each other off, quickly, without belaboring it, but it still feels so, so good. It's Hunter doing it, Hunter touching him, and that thought makes Devin stiffen and cry into Hunter's mouth while his coordination goes a bit wonky, but Hunter doesn't seem to mind because almost as soon as Devin's done, Hunter's coming, hot and slick in Devin's hand.

Devin did that. He made Hunter come. He's breathing hard and he doesn't want to stop kissing Hunter because if he stops one of them is going to have to say something.

Eventually, the stickiness becomes impossible to ignore. A rock pokes uncomfortably into Devin's thigh. Hunter lays one last close-mouthed kiss on Devin before pulling away, wiping his hand on his terrible trousers. Devin almost wants to do it, too, just so they have even more of a reason to bin the damn things. But he fishes a handkerchief out of his pocket, cleans himself up, then offers the cloth to Hunter, who takes it without compunction and does the same. A minute later they're both zipped away and struggling to do up the buttons of their shirts.

"Fuck it," Devin says. "I give up. I'm putting them in the wrong holes anyway."

Hunter chuckles and lets his shirt hang open, too. "I think I lost my tie."

"My tie, you mean."

"Your tie." He pauses and adds, "Sorry."

Devin's suddenly terrified that he's not apologizing for the tie. "Don't be. I have others."

"But that was a nice one."

"Hunter, I don't care about the tie."

"Okay. Thanks."

Now Devin doesn't know what he's thanking him for. "Don't mention it."

"Is that—" Hunter stops, clears his throat. Devin wishes he could make out his expression in the dark, but there's too many shadows. "Is that what you want to do—not mention it?"

Devin feels cold. "Um. I." So here they are, then, and so quickly. But he's not going to lie, not when he just had his tongue down Hunter's throat and Hunter seemed to be enjoying the hell out of it. "No, not really. I'm okay with...mentioning it."

"I don't—I'm really no good at this sort of thing, Devin."

"Well I thought you were fairly decent," he says lightly. Trying to make it a joke.

Hunter doesn't rise to the bait. "You know what I mean. I wasn't being self-deprecating when I said I was grumpy and difficult and all that. I'm a bad bargain."

Devin wants to tell Hunter that he doesn't care. He's known Hunter for years and put up with him in all kinds of moods and he still wakes up every morning wanting Hunter's face to be the one he sees first. But Hunter's suddenly up off the ground and jogging—no—*running* down the hill.

Devin's not fast enough to catch him.

SEVENTEEN

FUCK. *Fuck. Fuck. Fuck. Fuck. Fuck.*

It's pretty much the only word Hunter's brain can conjure up as he takes off at a dead run down the dark hillside toward the lights of the party. His night vision is more than decent, and his sense of direction is uncanny. He still feels lost.

He stops just outside the barn, only a little winded from the run, uncomfortably aware of the state of his clothes. He glances down at himself. His belt's too loose and his shirt is unbuttoned. His fingers are shaking so hard he gives up with half the buttons still undone.

Fuck.

What did he do? He and Devin—they were never supposed to—and now Hunter has—and everything's wrong and—

He scrubs a hand over his eyes, turns away from the party, heading for the road. He should just leave, save everyone from having to endure his pathetic little breakdown because he couldn't resist Devin standing on a hilltop, starlight making his eyes shine. Because Hunter was too selfish to stop himself from kissing his best friend. From touching him. From taking.

He'd go back to Myrna and Gary's, but Devin has the keys to the rental car, and that's where Devin will end up anyway. He feels like running more—maybe he should just run all the way to California like Forrest Gump. Yeah, that's a good plan. He'll run until his feet bleed and he can't think about how much of an idiot he is.

It must be going on midnight, but there's no reason not to get started. He's well away from the barn now, passing the parking lot, when he hears his name.

"Hunter, what are you doing?"

Not Devin. Jillian. He looks in the direction of the voice, and there she is, his ex-wife, Dr. Jillian Meade, the best pediatric oncologist in the country, leaning against the hood of a black SUV in her wedding dress. Smoking a cigarette.

"I thought you quit."

"I did." She takes a drag and looks at the remainder, offers it to Hunter. "You want the rest? I didn't really need one. Just needed a second to myself."

Hunter waves the offering away. She drops it onto the gravel and steps on it with her delicate high heel.

"You okay, Jill?"

"I'm exhausted. This whole wedding thing has given me a new appreciation for how you and I eloped." She laughs, throaty and wry. "What are you doing out here? Where's Devin? And why do you look like your dog died?"

"I don't have a dog," Hunter says.

"It's a figure of speech, Hunter."

Hunter doesn't know what to tell her, so he changes the subject. "It was a beautiful wedding. Aaron's a lucky guy."

Jillian smiles. She does look a little tired, but not unhappy. Hunter's heart eases slightly, until he hears the next thing out of her mouth. "So is Devin."

Hunter closes his eyes in defeat. He should have known this was coming from the moment Devin's name left his mouth weeks ago. "I have to tell you something. Devin and I—we're not together. I asked him to pretend to be dating me so you wouldn't think I was some pathetic mess who can't get a date to a wedding, even though I am, and he said he would, because he's the nicest guy in the world, but something went wrong, besides lying to you and your family and everyone I mean, because we—we're *friends*, but I screwed up and I'm so sorry, Jill."

He opens his eyes and Jillian's still there, forehead wrinkled. "You and Devin aren't together?"

"No."

"Then why do you look like you've just been thoroughly debauched? And don't try to lie, Hunter, I know what you look like after sex. Not to mention you have grass in your hair and you're missing a few buttons on your shirt."

"Well, we just did some stuff. It was the first time. Our first time."

The forehead wrinkles disappear. "And how was it?"

Hunter doesn't know how to answer the question. It had felt like nothing he'd experienced before, so exciting and new and yet familiar, because it was Devin, the person he feels safest with in the entire world. Kissing him, touching him, was like—freedom. But then it was over, and Hunter had to face the fact that his only long-term relationship was with a woman who'd just married someone else and he was only going to end up hurting Devin, screwing it up in some way, and lose his best friend in the process. So he decided to get the ball rolling on that as quickly as possible and ran.

But since he can't explain all of that to Jillian and she's apparently still waiting for an answer, he just says, "Good."

"You did 'stuff' with your best friend and it was good. I'm not understanding why you're skulking away in the middle of my wedding reception. And sulking, too."

"I'm not sulking," Hunter says, though even he can hear the distinctly sulky undertone to his voice. He glares at her. "I'm just doing him a favor. Devin deserves so much better than me."

"Don't you think he should be able to decide that for himself?"

Her words echo Devin's own from earlier in the night. Hunter shrugs. "I'm no good for anyone. You know that."

Jillian takes a step forward and puts her arm around Hunter. "Hunter, honey, you are the most incredible man I've ever known. Aaron included. We didn't work out because you loved me with only one part of your heart, the part that missed your parents and your childhood and the time before you went to some really dark places. You needed me then. But you need Devin now. And something tells me you love him with more than one part of your heart."

"Love?" Hunter has trouble even getting out the word. He doesn't love Devin. Does he?

"You've talked about the man nonstop for three years and when I finally get to meet him, you look at him with hearts in your eyes. He looks at you the exact same way. That must be why I had no idea you were lying about being with him. You're a good liar, Hunter, but not that good. And he must care about you an awful lot to agree to put on a charade like that."

"He—he's the best." Suddenly there's a lump in Hunter's throat that makes it hard to breathe, let alone talk. He takes one shaky breath, then another before he can say, "Jillian, I do need him. He's the best part of my day, every day. I hate Mondays because those are his days off. We built SkyTrip together and he always makes everything better. That's why I can't be with him. I can't love him. That would ruin everything."

"Not even if he loves you back?"

Hunter's about to say he can't. But he thinks about Devin tying his tie for him. Then untying it. He thinks about coffee and careful driving and duct tape. He thinks —*maybe*. And the merest possibility of it makes his heart ache with want.

"But how do I—" Hunter doesn't even know how to finish the sentence. He's completely out of his depth. His relationship with Jillian had been carried along on a wave of spontaneity and trauma avoidance. He and Devin are in a very different place.

Jillian grips his arm. "I believe in you, Hunter. You'll figure it out. I suggest you start by not running away."

"How did you know I was running away?"

"I know you." She leans over and kisses him on the cheek. "Now, go find your fake boyfriend and make him your real one."

Hunter's not so certain that's going to be as easy as it sounds.

EIGHTEEN

HUNTER'S not at the reception when Devin arrives back, breathing hard from his run—okay, it was more like a jog and maybe he's not in as good shape as he prides himself on—down the hill. The party looks to be winding down. The eighties band is packing their gear, having been replaced on the sound system by trendy, grating music from someone's phone. A few couples are still sticking it out on the dance floor, while the catering staff clear off the mostly empty tables.

Devin takes a detour to the table he and Hunter had shared to grab his jacket and waistcoat. He checks the pockets and finds the car keys intact. He glances at Hunter's coat and hesitates, torn. It's not really his place to decide one way or another. But then again if Hunter wanted it back, he'd have returned for it, wouldn't he? Devin leaves it, after patting it down to make sure nothing valuable is being left behind.

The bartender is closing the bar but gives Devin a bottle of water upon request. He feels sober, but his head's starting to ache, and he doesn't want to take any chances. He leans with his back to the bar as he drains the bottle. Hunter's not here. Devin tries not to panic. Just because Hunter had run away after they—Devin tries to figure out the proper way to describe what happened. They didn't fuck, and they didn't make love. He settles on fooled around. That feels accurate—he's definitely a fool if nothing else.

So just because Hunter literally ran away after they fooled around doesn't mean he regrets it. Maybe he just remembered he had to be someplace and didn't have time to wait for Devin. He smacks himself in the forehead with the empty water bottle. And maybe they've just screwed up their friendship by screwing around in the dark like teenagers.

Part of him wants to find Hunter, and another part of him wants Hunter to find him. This entire weekend Devin's bent over backward to be the person that Hunter wanted him to be. And what has he gotten for his troubles? Abandoned at a wedding with grass stains on his expensive trousers.

He's determined to start making his own decisions from here on out. No more deference to Hunter's whims, no more confusing gray area between friend and pseudo-lover. If he wants to be with Hunter, he should just tell him so. And if Hunter doesn't want to be with Devin, well, then. Devin's a grownup. He'll deal.

Of course, there is SkyTrip to consider. And those unsigned partnership papers Devin figured could wait until they got back from New York. Will Hunter still want him to sign them? Will Devin be able to go on working day in and day out with Hunter now that he knows what he sounds like when he comes? Can his heart heal up if he's in constant contact with the man he can't have?

He straightens his spine, tosses the water bottle in a recycling container, and marches toward the car park. He's worked with Hunter every day for three years with an unrequited crush. He can jolly well keep working with him even if this one night is all they'll ever be to each other. Hunter's still on friendly terms with lots of his one-night stands. Devin's in good company he thinks wryly.

His step falters as he considers what might happen if Hunter finds someone to be with for more than a night. To see him with another person, to see him smile at them, laugh with them. To take them up in the air in one of SkyTrip's planes, Hunter behind the controls, something Hunter's offered to do with him dozens of times. Devin's always been too chicken. Large planes are bad enough. Small planes make him break out in goosebumps. Ironic, of course, given the company he's spent three years of his life dedicated to. But no doubt Hunter's next relationship will be with someone who's not afraid of flying.

And Devin will be stuck on the ground. Alone.

He makes his way through the nearly empty lot to find the rental SUV. Jillian and Aaron's car is gone. He didn't really say goodbye, but considering he'd never met them before two days ago, he supposes that's acceptable. He takes one last look around in case Hunter's waiting for him, but there's no one. He gets in the car and drives back to Jillian's parents'. The lights are on, and he hears voices in the kitchen, but he heads straight up to the guest room, unwilling to have to pretend everything's okay. Pretending feels like all he's done this weekend and he's no good at it anyway. He strips off his clothes, leaves them in a heap on the floor, and climbs into bed in his boxers. He tells himself he's too tired to shower, but as he falls asleep, he knows he doesn't want to wash the smell of Hunter off him quite yet.

NINETEEN

HUNTER'S FEET HURT.

After kissing Jillian goodbye, literally, he hiked back up to the top of the Atkins Farm hill to try to find Devin's tie, finally locating it but draining his phone's battery using the flashlight feature in the process, then trudged down again only to find Devin—and their vehicle—gone. So he'd hit the road on foot after all, walking on the side of the highway in his dress shoes.

He's still a mile away from Myrna and Gary's and he may have survived boot camp and Afghanistan and several other terrifying places, but his feet still hurt. He's a civilian now. He's allowed to complain about his feet.

The pain isn't quite enough to distract him from his thoughts, which aren't exactly a picnic, either. Jillian had been so certain of herself when she'd calmly suggested that Devin and he could find a path forward together. It's easy for her to say, having known Devin for all of two days and only having seen them when they're pretending to be a couple.

Of course, it's not like he'd had to stretch himself the last couple of days. He'd had a great time being with Devin outside of work, talking to him about real stuff, having him around in the morning for his first cup of coffee and falling asleep in bed next to him at night. If Hunter thought Devin would want to keep all of that going when they get back home—he swallows hard, trying to imagine Devin in his tiny trailer with the broken coffee maker and dodgy truck. His face burns with the inadequacy of it all. Devin should have the world— maybe someone like that Sean guy who probably has a big house and a Porsche and a golden retriever and would make love to Devin on a king-sized bed with soft fancy sheets.

The idea of Devin with anyone else, fancy sheets or no, makes him speed up his gait. But it doesn't matter how jealous Hunter is or how much he wants to be the guy that puts a smile on his friend's face first thing in the morning and last thing at night, he's not allowed to have that. Devin's too smart to sign up for a relationship with Hunter. It doesn't matter what Jillian thinks is or isn't there. The plain fact is that Hunter can't have Devin and the sooner he faces it up to it the sooner everything can get back to normal.

There's light edging the trees on Bayberry Street when he finally reaches his destination. He notes with some relief that their rental car is there. Devin's inside, safe and sound. He hopes someone left the front door unlocked—he's a little too tired to pick the lock. Luckily, it swings open under his hand. The house is still and quiet. He takes off his shoes, creeps on stocking feet up to the guest room, trying not to disturb anyone.

Devin's asleep in the bed, illuminated by the gray dawn light coming around the edges of the blinds. He looks exhausted. He's entitled; he spent the last three days taking care of Hunter. That stops now.

Hunter eyes the empty side of the bed longingly, but he doesn't let himself drop into it and wrap his arms around Devin like he wants. Instead, he slips out of his clothes. He puts the suit pants in the trash basket. Step one in making all of this up to Devin. He doesn't want to risk waking Devin by taking a shower, so he dons a pair of jeans, throws the rest of his stuff into his suitcase as quietly as he can. Then he rolls up the borrowed tie and puts it on the bedside table. After a moment's hesitation, he grabs a piece of scrap paper and a pen and puts a few words down, slipping the paper under the tie.

He goes into the bathroom to collect his toiletries. He avoids his reflection in the mirror. He knows what he'll see. Circles under sad eyes, flyaway hair. No smile. The only joy in what he's about to do is knowing it's the best thing for Devin.

It takes only a minute to gather up his stuff from the bathroom, wash his hands, and carefully ease open the door. He doesn't look at the bed, keeps his head down as he stuffs his things in the outer pocket of his bag.

"What the hell are you doing?" It's Devin, voice rough, sitting up in bed. He's shirtless, and he's holding Hunter's note.

"I'm leaving."

"Running away, you mean."

He deserves the scorn in Devin's voice, but it still hurts. "I made a mess of this whole weekend, and I'm sorry. I thought it would be better if—"

"If you left me in the middle of the night? Is this supposed to be some kind of goodbye note? 'Thanks for the loan. E.'" He waves the piece of paper Hunter left by the tie. "Don't your other one-night stands get a proper goodbye, or do you just sneak out of their beds, too?"

Is that what Devin thinks he is? A one-night stand? "No, listen, it's not like that. I'm sorry, and I know this must look like I'm a coward, but I'm just trying to make things the way they were."

"The way they were? When, Hunter? Before you dragged me here to play house with you or before we got each other off? Or maybe before we met? Is that it—do you want me to quit SkyTrip?"

"Jesus, no. Of course not. SkyTrip is just as much yours as mine." Hunter can't imagine SkyTrip without Devin. He can't imagine life without him, full stop, but he's messing this up so badly that seems like a real possibility.

"So why are you going?" Now Devin's voice just sounds sad. "We can still be friends, can't we? I get that you regret the other stuff, but we can forget it happened. Chalk it up to the wild stuff people do at their ex's weddings and yeah, go on as we were before. I guess."

Hunter gapes at Devin. He sounds so sad, yet Hunter knows with certainty that Devin means what he's saying. He doesn't know where to start. "First of all, I don't regret it. I mean, I do, but not the way you might mean. And second of all, you'd do that? Just forget it. Does our friendship mean that much to you?" Hunter doesn't know if he should hug Devin or smack him on the head for being so devoted to Hunter when he clearly doesn't deserve it.

"*You* mean that much to me, Hunter." Devin closes his eyes tiredly, then opens them and says flatly, "I'm in love with you."

Hunter sways on his feet. He hasn't slept in nearly twenty-four hours and the last thing he ate was some couscous salad from the wedding reception buffet. He can't be hearing Devin right.

In a flash, Devin's out of bed and at Hunter's elbow, grabbing his arm and saying, "Steady on, Hunter. Sit down, come on. You all right?"

Devin helps him to the bed, and he sinks down. The wave of dizziness passes. "I'm fine." He bats Devin's hands away, but he doesn't go far, sitting down next to Hunter on the edge of the bed. "You look really pale. Let me get you some water."

"No!"

Devin freezes at Hunter's tone.

"You're always doing things for me. Always taking care of me. Don't you know I'm not worth it?"

"Hunter, stop this right now. You're allowed to not love me back, but you aren't allowed to tell me how to feel. I like doing things for you, you stupid man. And maybe I'm stupid for doing it even when you could never feel the same way about me. But if there's anything good to come out of this pretend boyfriend nonsense it's that I finally told you— well, I don't want you to think I was pining away after you or anything, because I wasn't, I mean, if all we ever are is friends that's completely fine—but at the end of the day the truth is, Hunter, that I've fancied you for a long time."

Devin sighs and goes on before Hunter can fully absorb all of that. "And you may not think so, but you've always been there for me, too. So please stop with the self- pity and the self-deprecation. You can't hide the person you are. Jillian knows it, her entire family knows it, and Louis and Will and Isabelle and Laney—they know it, too. You're a good person, Hunter Pike. And you're very much loved. Platonically. And non-platonically, at least in my case. Can't speak for the others, but I'd imagine there are one or two others who'd give you a go if you asked."

Hunter can't help smiling faintly as Devin's speech ends on a little joke. God, even in the darkest moments Devin makes Hunter feel better.

"You're so much braver than I am," he says.

Devin scoffs. "So says the man who leaps from airplanes without a second thought."

"I mean it. You can just say all that stuff and face the consequences. I, for some reason, I'm terrified to tell you —" he stops, his words caught in his throat. He feels dizzy again. He's only dimly aware of Devin leaving, and then coming back moments later with a paper cup of water. Devin holds the cup to his lips. He takes a small sip. Devin sits with him until the water is gone.

"See what I mean?"

"You're exhausted, Hunter. Where were you all night, anyway?"

"I went back to the hill where we—and I found your tie. And then I walked back here."

"But that's at least ten miles!" Devin looks horrified.

Hunter shrugs. It seemed to make sense at the time. "Maybe I could just lie down for a few minutes before I get out of your hair."

Devin opens his mouth, then seems to think better of whatever the was going to say. He nods. "Yeah. Scoot back and take a nap."

"Just a few minutes," Hunter says, shuffling back on the bed until his head hits the pillow. He closes his eyes. He thinks he can feel the press of Devin's lips to his temple and hear him whisper something, but he's asleep before he can figure out what Devin said.

TWENTY

WHEN HUNTER WAKES UP, the room is bathed in gray light. He must have only been asleep for a few minutes. Strange that his mouth should feel dry as the desert on which SkyTrip sits. With effort, he wrenches his arm around to the front of his face and squints at his watch in the semi-darkness. A little before seven. He blinks and yawns and swings his feet down to the floor. His bag is still where he left it, but Devin's suitcase is missing. He feels the first stirrings of panic. Nothing about this is right. He was only asleep for half an hour or so. Devin can't have gone far.

He'd had the strangest dream, though. Devin told him he was in love with him and that he'd felt that way for a long time. And Hunter had—had almost passed out. Wait. That part wasn't a dream. *Oh my god.* Devin loves him.

And his suitcase is gone.

Hunter throws on his boots, grabs his phone, which someone thoughtfully had plugged into the charger, and flies down the stairs. If Devin only just left Hunter should be able to find him before he takes off for home. But if Devin has the car, how will Hunter get to the airport?

He's about to track down Myrna or Gary and beg them to let him use one of their vehicles, when he hears voices from the kitchen. He makes a beeline there, and stops dead in the doorway, trying to make sense of what he sees.

Myrna and Gary are indeed there. So is Devin. They're all at the kitchen bar eating pizza. The grease-stained box from Capelli's sits on the counter. Myrna's got a glass of red wine and Devin's got a glass of white. The three of them are chatting, but Devin's laughter at something Gary just said dies in his throat when he catches sight of Hunter.

"You're up," he says, his voice studiedly neutral.

Hunter's brain is working at a snail's pace. "Either you're eating pizza for breakfast or it's not seven A.M."

"It's not Opposite Day," Devin says with a hint of a smile. "You've been asleep all day."

"I slept for twelve hours?" Impossible. He's never slept that much at once in his life.

"You must have needed it," Devin says. "And you must be starving. There's more pizza."

Hunter suddenly realizes how hungry he is. And how confused. If he's been asleep all day, what has Devin been doing? Where's Devin's suitcase? And why is he having dinner with Myrna and Gary like he does it five nights a week? Well, he's not going to solve all these mysteries on an empty stomach. He shrugs, grabs three slices of loaded pie, gets himself a glass of water, and takes the only remaining seat which is next to Devin.

Devin gives him a tentative smile when he sits down. Hunter owes him so much more than a smile back, but it's a start. Devin seems relieved to see Hunter's expression and goes back to eating his pizza.

A cell phone buzzes loudly on the bar top, and Myrna checks the screen. "It's a text from Jillian. They're at the resort."

"Oh good. Give her my love," Gary says. "And tell her to send some pictures once in a while."

"You know she's terrible at pictures," Myrna says, tapping away at her screen.

"That's why she needs the reminder."

"Give her our best, too," Hunter says. He feels slightly more normal after inhaling a slice of pizza and half the water. It's only after his mouth is full of another bite that he realizes how his phrasing sounds. He and Devin aren't an "our." Or at least not until they get some privacy to talk all this out.

"So, when's your flight again?" Gary asks. "You need to leave plenty of time at the airport—traffic can be a nightmare."

Hunter's mouth is full again, and Devin answers. "Er —we were booked on the six P.M. flight tomorrow, but I called and there's space on the morning flight if we wanted to go back early."

"Nonsense," Myrna says before Hunter can respond. "We haven't gotten to see nearly enough of you and who knows when we'll be able to drag Hunter back to Apple Vale again. Tomorrow morning we'll all go out for breakfast and then you two could fit in a hike, maybe, up to Bald Rock, or at least another swim before—"

"Or maybe you can let them plan their own itinerary, dear?" Gary says lightly. "I know it's hard to believe, but Hunter's not a teenager anymore."

She smiles wryly. "I know that. But I'm allowed to be a little mother hennish. Now that Jillian and Aaron are putting down roots in the city, and Rick and Anna are settled with little Kai—well, my motherly energy has to go somewhere. Maybe we should get a dog."

Gary grumbles around his bite. "A dog! What about traveling? How can we visit Hunter and Devin in California with a dog to worry about?"

"Oh, that's a wonderful idea! And long overdue." She gives Gary a kiss on the cheek. "I knew I married you for a reason."

He rolls his eyes, but Hunter doesn't miss the slight blush on the sixty-five -year-old's cheeks. He feels a stab of envy at their casual intimacy. Thirty-odd years married and they can still tease each other and put a blush on the other's face. He wonders if his parents would be equally as happy at this stage of their marriage. His father was a good ten years older than Gary—would he have gotten grumpy and curmudgeonly in his old age? Would his mother have been exasperated or fond? He likes to think they'd still be as in love as he remembers them.

"We'd love to have you, anytime," Devin says. "I can give you the tour of SkyTrip—at least on the ground level. Hunter can take you up in the air if you'd like. The desert is actually quite beautiful from ten thousand feet, especially if you go at dawn or sunset."

"Do you go up, often, Devin?" Myrna asks.

Hunter answers for him. "I've never been able to get him up there with me."

"I'm not the best flyer," Devin admits. "But I've seen pictures the others have brought back."

They talk about the merits of flying smaller planes versus airline travel for a while, until the pizza is entirely consumed and Hunter's gotten his equilibrium back, at least as far as rest and nutrition are concerned. He could use a shower. And though his nerves jangle every time he thinks about the conversation he and Devin need to have, he can't put it off any longer.

"I know I've been sleeping all day, but I'm still kind of beat. Is it okay if Devin and I turn in early?"

Devin looks at him, surprised, but Gary and Myrna just wave them away. "We'll take care of cleanup. We'll plan on breakfast at the Apple Pan—around eight?"

"Fine." Hunter would agree to anything in order to escape back upstairs. "See you then." He grabs Devin by the arm and pulls him gently but firmly toward the stairs. "Where's your suitcase?" he whispers.

"I put it in the other guest room," Devin says.

"Why?"

"Well, I didn't want to disturb you for one thing. And I didn't think you'd want to have to share with me, especially not if there was an extra bed in the house. All the other houseguests have gone."

Devin proves, as always, to be more thoughtful than Hunter gives him credit for. "Do they know—did you tell Myrna and Gary that we're not—"

"No," Devin cuts in. "I didn't think it was my place. I

just told Gary that I wanted you to be able to get more sleep, so I might take one of the other beds. He didn't seem to think anything of it."

Hunter knows he'll have to tell them eventually, but that's a problem for future Hunter. They're back in the room they've been sharing for the past three days. He shuts the door, then locks it. He switches on the bedside lamp, turns back to Devin.

"We need to talk."

TWENTY-ONE

DEVIN BITES BACK A SARCASTIC RETORT. Of course they need to talk. But at least Hunter's gotten here eventually. Still, he swallows nervously. It remains to be seen what Hunter thinks they need to talk about. Is this the final blow—the conversation that kills the last shred of hope Devin might be holding that the two of them have any chance whatsoever?

After Hunter passed out cold that morning, Devin had made sure he was comfortable, gathered his things, and retreated to the ground floor. He hadn't had the best night's sleep ever, but at least he'd slept while Hunter was marching around the countryside in dress shoes and hating himself. He'd spent the day on his laptop, catching up on SkyTrip business and looking in on Hunter every couple of hours. He'd also checked the flight itineraries home. He wanted to be ready in case Hunter ends up needing space. Or he does. He had begun to realize that even though he's told himself he'll be fine if Hunter doesn't return his feelings, he needs to prepare himself for the very real possibility that he'll be going back to work at SkyTrip nursing a broken a heart.

Hunter's been pacing back and forth in their small bedroom. His hair is comically mussed, there's stubble on his cheeks, and he's still wearing his dress shirt from the wedding. He looks adorable. Devin leans his head to the side and asks, "So, what did you want to talk about?" He wants to make this easier on Hunter, but he's still acutely aware that wanting to make things easy for Hunter is partly what's gotten them into this situation.

"When I woke up today, I thought it was a dream."

Hunter's still pacing and Devin supposes he should let him burn off his extra energy, but he's not the one who slept all day, so he sits down on the edge of the bed and leans back on his arms.

"You thought what was a dream?"

"You telling me you're in love with me."

Devin cringes slightly. He'd thought maybe Hunter was so out of it he wouldn't remember. Not that he would have wanted to have to say it again. It had hurt enough the first time. But it had also been freeing. A bit like lancing a wound—painful, but necessary. Maybe a broken heart is the first step toward recovery.

"No, not a dream," he says lightly.

Hunter stops pacing and stands still a foot in front of Devin. Devin tips his head up to meet Hunter's gaze. His expression is unreadable, but his voice is gravel rough when he says, "So you— you really...."

Devin's usual M.O. would be to jump in and finish Hunter's sentence but he's trying to do things differently.

Hunter's a grownup. He can finish his own emotionally complicated sentences.

"...feel that way about me?" Hunter finally says.

"Yes." Devin's pulse leaps as he says the word. But he's past the point of denying it—to Hunter or to himself.

Hunter sucks in a breath at his answer. "Okay. Uh. I'm sorry I fell asleep instead of responding like a normal person."

"Well, you were tired. And I gather from your statement that you don't think you're normal. Didn't we have a talk about the self-deprecation? Or did you think that was a dream, too?"

Hunter shrugs awkwardly. "I think I'm going to have to work on it."

Devin wants to cheer. That alone is progress. "Well, I have to agree. You're not the most normal person I know, actually. You're pretty extraordinary."

Hunter runs a hand through his hair, messing it up even more. "How can you just say stuff like that?"

Suddenly, Devin worries he's making Hunter uncomfortable. He puts a hand up. "Sorry, I got carried away for a second. I know you don't want me to act differently. We're friends and I think it's important to both of us that we're able to stay friends. Though, as your friend, I believe I'm still allowed to think you're extraordinary."

"I do want to be your friend," Hunter says slowly.

Devin closes his eyes. Of course. He should be pleased. At least Hunter doesn't want to cut him out of his life, out of their business. "Right. Well. Good." He'd say more but he's trying to keep his breathing under control. For some reason he feels like crying.

The bed dips next to him as Hunter sits down. He forces his eyes open and Hunter's close. Much closer than he expected.

"But I was hoping, when we get home, that you might want to have dinner with me sometime?"

Hunter's eyes are so near Devin can pick out the different shades of green, can see the pupil get bigger when he turns his head away from the lamplight.

"Dinner? Didn't we just have dinner?"

"That wasn't a proper date."

"Date?" Devin feels like he missed something. Wasn't Hunter trying to let him down easily? When did they start talking about dates?

"I'd very much like to take you out to dinner. Just the two of us. No extended family. No exes. No audience. Just you and me. If you want to." Hunter sounds like he thinks Devin might say no, which is ridiculous, but Devin does need one thing cleared up before he can answer.

"Why do you want to take me to dinner, Hunter?"

"Because I like you very much. As a friend, yes, but also, as you put it last night—or this morning, I guess— non-platonically. As in, romantically." He pauses a second and Devin can see his throat work as he swallows. "Sexually."

Now Devin feels like the one who's in a dream. "Ah. Well then. I accept. I'd love to go to dinner with you."

"You would?" Hunter's a bit disbelieving.

"Of course. If you really mean it." Suddenly, Devin's worried that Hunter's just trying to do what he thinks Devin wants and he's not actually attracted to him at all. "You do—don't you?"

Hunter pushes up off the bed and starts pacing again. "Look, I know we're doing this all upside-down and backward, and I'm sorry, but that's just the way it happened and a little while ago when I thought you'd left me I realized just how big of an idiot I've been trying to talk myself out of something that I'm incredibly lucky to have in the first place. Something I thought I'd never have again."

He takes a beat to breathe and keeps going as if he's afraid to stop. "I fell for my best friend, and I was too blind to realize it was happening. I think it's been happening since the moment I saw you in that Starbucks and you smiled at me and made me feel like I could do anything in the world. No one else has ever made me feel like that, Devin. Only you. And when I proposed this whole wedding date thing, I didn't realize that being close to you would feel so good, that being with you would make me so happy. Being happy scares me."

Devin's been following Hunter's pacing with his gaze while he talks and he's a little dizzy. He pats the bed beside him. Hunter sits down obediently. "Why does being happy scare you?" He thinks he knows the answer, but he wonders if Hunter does.

"Being happy is just a prelude to having something taken away. My parents. My fellow soldiers. Jillian. You and SkyTrip are the best things that have ever happened to me. I was scared that if I let myself really ask for what I wanted, then something bad was going to happen. I Iell, maybe I still think it might. But that's not fair to you. And maybe it's something I can work on."

Devin's so proud of Hunter he can feel his heart

expand in his chest cavity. "Loving sometimes does mean losing, Hunter. But I'm here to stay. And we can work on it together."

"I like the sound of that." And then Hunter smiles, the big, bright smile that captivated Devin from day one.

"So, does this mean we have to wait until our proper date to have a goodnight kiss?" he asks, shifting the mood from serious to playful.

Hunter's gaze flicks to Devin's mouth. "Well, considering we've already had our first kiss, I don't know that we have to wait."

"Our first kiss wasn't real," Devin reminds him.

"It was real, Devin. I just didn't know it at the time. But we can have a do-over if you like."

"You're right, it was real. This is real, too, as much as it seems like a fantasy come to life." Devin reaches out and puts his hand around the back of Hunter's neck, draws him in close, as if to prove to them both that this is really happening.

Hunter comes easily, his skin warm against Devin's palm, the hair at the nape of his neck brushing the back of Devin's hand. He leans in and kisses Hunter openmouthed. Hunter groans and slips his tongue against Devin's. They trade long, wet, deep kisses that leave Devin tingling from head to toe and Hunter straining against him, trying to get closer even though they've got clothes very much in the way.

Devin finally pulls away to inspect Hunter, whose mouth is red and swollen. "This is real," he says again. Hunter's so perfect, so everything he's wanted for so long, he says it to convince himself as much as Hunter.

Hunter nods, then his expression grows sly. "And I really need to see you naked."

Devin coughs and laughs at the same time. "Seriously? In your in-laws' house?"

Hunter shrugs. "Ex-in-laws. And they probably think we've fucked every night we've been here."

The notion had honestly not occurred to Devin. He decides being naked with the man he loves is more important than any embarrassment he's going to feel at breakfast in the morning.

"Well in that case. You first."

Hunter raises his eyebrows.

"Strip, Mr. Pike."

TWENTY-TWO

HUNTER LOOKS AT DEVIN, who's smiling at him confidently. "Excuse me?"

"Take off your clothes."

Hunter's dick jumps unexpectedly at the note of command in Devin's voice. Huh. He'll think about the implications of that later. But instead of complying he says, "I could use a shower."

"Well, unless you take your showers fully clothed, I don't see the problem." Then he leans back and crosses his arms, as if waiting for Hunter to get on with it.

Hunter's not particularly self-conscious about his body. He and Devin have seen each other in nothing more than swim trunks in just the last couple of days. Not to mention the fact they had their hands on each other's cocks less than twenty-four hours ago. But this is different. This is...intentional nudity. As Hunter unbuttons his filthy white dress shirt and peels it off, he does it knowing Devin wants to see him like this, that he's cataloging every muscle, every scar. Devin's eyes are glued to him, in fact, and the fact that Devin's so into it spurs Hunter on. He bends over to unlace his boots, feeling Devin's gaze on his bent over back as acutely as if he had his hands all over him.

He takes a bit more time shimmying his jeans off. He has a pair of black briefs on underneath, and he stands in just those for a minute, letting Devin's gaze roam his body. He wasn't lying about needing that shower, but he doesn't feel unclean under Devin's careful eye. He feels kind of reborn, as if this is their first time all over again. As if this is his first time again. It's the first time he's had sex with someone he was in love with, outside of Jillian, and this time isn't about hanging onto the past or desperately searching for something to live for. Being with Devin is about the future, not the past. It's about the life he's built out of desert sand and airplane fuel and grease and sweat. It's about the life they've built together.

Before he shucks off his underwear, he realizes he hasn't told Devin the bit about being in love with him yet. He's honestly terrified to take this last step, but he also feels strong. Devin's with him. And Devin's not going to let him fall, not without a chute.

"I love you," he says, firm and clear. He doesn't want there to be any mistake.

Devin's eyes grow wide. "I love you, too." They hold eye contact for one long beat. Two. Then Devin smirks. "Show me what you got, hot stuff."

Hunter cracks, huffing out a laugh and thumbing the waistband of his briefs down over his hips. He's been half hard since making out with Devin on the bed, and his cock hangs heavy and thick between his legs. Devin looks at Hunter like he's starving and Hunter is the last slice of pizza. He feels himself filling out under Devin's gaze. He cups his balls, strokes himself a couple of times. The way Devin's eyes close to slits and his mouth parts with want makes Hunter fully hard in a matter of seconds.

"God, how did I not realize how sexy your mouth is?" Hunter says. His voice sounds breathy to his ears, but he doesn't care. He's so turned on right now he feels like he could come just stroking himself dry while Devin watches.

Devin doesn't say anything, just licks his lips and the sight of Devin's tongue makes Hunter's cock jerk responsively.

"You want to take that shower now?" He's trying to be cool, but there's an unmistakable note of begging in his question.

But Devin's not done teasing him. He nods, then takes his own sweet time undressing. First his Pavement shirt comes off, and Hunter's gaze skips between the Tardis tattoo and his dusky pink nipples. His mouth waters. What he wouldn't give to have his mouth on those. Later, he promises himself. Devin toes off his sneakers and socks and has his hands on his fly but stops before unzipping.

Hunter groans. "You're killing me, babe."

Devin's hands drop to the sides.

Wrong direction Hunter's brain screams.

"Babe?" Devin asks.

"Uh. Is that not good?" The endearment had kind of slipped out. He'd never called Jillian babe —she'd been

Jill or honey, occasionally. But maybe Devin isn't ready to move their relationship to the pet names level so soon.

"No, it's okay," Devin says. "I am a pretty hot babe."

"Well, I think so." And it's true. He may have worked alongside Devin for three years and not realized exactly how attractive he was, but he'd always noticed his clear, honest eyes, his charming laugh, the appealingly competent way his fingers fly across his keyboard. Okay, Hunter's an idiot for not realizing what all that meant. But he's there now. And he wants nothing more than to show Devin exactly how hot he finds him. Through gritted teeth he says, "Please take off the rest of your clothes and come over here."

Devin finally takes mercy and after a few deft motions his jeans and boxers drop to the floor. He steps out of them and Hunter can finally appreciate Devin's entire slender but strong body. His cock, flushed rosy pink, rises from dark blond curls. Devin walks toward him without hesitation, steps right up into Hunter's personal space, wraps his arms around him and pulls him in for a deep, heady kiss.

Kissing Devin on the bed fully clothed had felt pretty fucking awesome, but kissing him like this, their naked bodies pressed together from thigh to chest, mouths locked—Hunter's very soul feels engulfed in a flame of desire that seems like it will never be quenched. He needs Devin like breathing. He doesn't know how long they pass like that—it could be minutes, it could be hours —but eventually they break apart long enough for Devin to murmur, "God, I love you, Hunter Pike." And Hunter comes, with just the pressure of Devin's lean muscle against his swollen cock. He can't help the overwhelming sensation of rightness, of pleasure that courses through him. He chases the ropes of come pulsing out of him with his hand, trying to catch them so as not to make a mess of the guest room carpet.

"Fuck," he pants. "Sorry. I—"

"Please don't ever apologize for an orgasm, Hunter," Devin says. And then he kisses him, soft and sweet.

The only thing Hunter can think to say is, "I love you." So he does. And Devin kisses him again.

EVENTUALLY, they make it to the shower, where Hunter gets a second wind and sucks Devin off quickly enough to bolster his ego for round two, which once they've washed each other's hair and basically dicked around in the shower long enough that the water starts to run cold, consists of Hunter making use of Devin's hastily retrieved lube and condoms to finger him open while sucking him hard again, then fucking him against the bathroom counter from behind while they stare into each other's eyes in the mirror.

Devin comes with a strangled cry all over the porcelain sink, and Hunter follows soon after, emptying himself into Devin, which is better than the biggest adrenaline high.

They collapse into the bed, naked and still damp from the shower and the washcloth they'd used to clean up after the bathroom sex. Devin yawns. "I know you probably couldn't sleep, but I'm worn out."

Hunter feels surprisingly tired even after his epic nap. "It's okay. I could sleep, I think. Either way, I'm not going anywhere."

"Good." Devin reaches over to turn off the light. For a second, Hunter's worried that he's going to retreat to his side of the bed. They might be in love and all, but who's to say that Devin likes to cuddle? But when he settles back down, he does so much closer to the middle of the bed than the edge, so Hunter happily scoots closer, wrapping an arm around Devin's waist.

He noses the back of Devin's neck, pressing a soft kiss there and Devin sighs.

"If this is a dream, I don't want to wake up," he says quietly.

"It's not a dream," Hunter says. "I promise."

"I love you," Devin says again. "I hope it's okay to keep saying it."

Hunter tightens his hold on Devin's waist. "It's okay. I probably need to hear it a few thousand times for it to really sink in. I'm such a lucky bastard."

"All right then. I love you."

"I love you, Devin."

Devin falls asleep first, but Hunter's not far behind. He dreams of pizza and flying and kisses that taste like home.

TWENTY-THREE

DEVIN WAKES up before Hunter for the first time since they got here. He can't believe they're flying home in just a few hours. Neither of them appears to have moved much in the night—they're both smack in the middle of the bed, Hunter's front molded to Devin's back. He scoots out from under Hunter's arm so he can shift and look at him. His hair is tangled over his forehead and he needs a shave. But he looks relaxed, content even, if Devin might venture to describe the peacefulness with which Hunter is sleeping.

He started to get over the sheer implausibility of Hunter being in love with him when he realized how much Hunter needs Devin's love. Devin's been at Hunter's side for three years, and he's only now grasping the many layers that have been hiding below Hunter's jaunty, confident exterior. That's all show. Underneath he's a man who's been hurt so badly that he's sealed himself off from true connection. He can't imagine what it's costing him to allow himself to be so vulnerable as to tell Devin he loves him.

Lucky for Hunter, Devin has no intention of being careless with Hunter's heart. They've been friends and business partners—becoming lovers is a miraculously wonderful development.

He checks the time and sees they'll have to get a move on if they're to meet Myrna and Gary for breakfast. He's debating whether it would be sweet or creepy to wake Hunter up by kissing him when Hunter's eyes open. They focus on Devin's face and then crinkle around the edges as Hunter smiles. "Hey."

"Hey. We need to get up for breakfast with the 'rents."

Hunter stretches and Devin gets an eyeful of warm, sheet-creased skin. "I don't suppose we have time for a quickie?"

Devin finds himself licking his lips and mentally calculating how fast he can get them to the diner. Myrna and Gary won't mind if they're a few minutes late, will they?

"A very quick quickie, I suppose." He grunts as Hunter grabs him around the waist and climbs on top of him, requiring no more encouragement than that. Heedless of morning breath or whiskers, he kisses Devin as if it's been years since they kissed rather than hours.

Devin arches into him, kissing back just as eagerly. When Hunter finally pulls back, Devin's achingly hard. Hunter wastes no time in getting them both in his hand, jerking them roughly off together, the motions erratic but hot all the same. Devin usually takes longer to come in the morning, but today with the man of his dreams touching him, looking at him like he's the best thing since the turbojet engine, he finds himself close fast. "Hunter—I'm going to—"

"Yeah, come on. You're so hot, babe. Wanna see you come." Hunter doesn't let up and he doesn't stop talking. "You're so gorgeous when you come. You feel so good. Fuck. Devin—I love you so much."

Devin's body tightens as he comes, violently. He's still coming down from the high as Hunter groans and adds to the mess on Devin's belly. Hunter doesn't seem to care about that as he drops down to kiss Devin, smearing the wet between them. Devin feels so incredible, so light-headed with love and coming before breakfast that it takes him a minute remember they're supposed to be getting ready, not making out.

"Time for another shower," he says breathlessly. "And you need a shave. Maybe I should text them that we'll be late."

"Very late," Hunter agrees, as he goes in for another kiss.

IT'S CLOSER to nine than eight when they finally walk into the Apple Pan, shaved, showered, and dressed. Devin can't get over how affectionate Hunter has been all morning—he might even use the word clingy if they weren't thirty-something adults. As they greet Myrna and Gary and slide into the booth opposite them, Hunter has his hand in Devin's the entire time, and when they sit, he settles in so their hips touch.

Devin suddenly remembers Jillian mentioning Hunter being slow to catch onto his feelings, but once he's there, being the sweetest guy in the world. He's never seen this side of Hunter before— affectionate, almost childishly open. He doesn't think it's only the afterglow. This is Hunter Pike in love.

If Devin hadn't fully realized the implications of that, it's beginning to sink in. This is his life now—or at least for as long as Hunter feels this way—he can touch, he can tease. They can have everything they had before and all of this, too. It's enough to make his chest hurt. It takes them ordering coffee —lots of coffee—and a mountain of food before he places the emotion. He's anxious. Having Hunter this way means that someday he could lose it, and that's a thought so devastating he feels his breathing getting shallow just contemplating it.

Even though he's managing to keep up his end of the conversation and consume more than his share of the coffee, he can't get rid of the nagging feeling of anxiety in his chest. He finds himself rubbing at his breastbone, as if he can massage it away.

Myrna and Gary don't seem to think anything is out of the ordinary. Hunter had decided not to tell them that he and Devin entered the wedding weekend as only pretend beaus—it would only cause confusion, and since they ended up together in the end Devin had agreed. But Hunter seems to notice that Devin is on edge, because he starts sending him concerned looks over the last bites of their omelets.

"Everything okay, babe?" he murmurs as Gary settles the bill.

Devin tries to draw in a complete breath and fails. "Um. I think I need some air."

"Guys, we're going to head out for that hike. Thanks for breakfast. We'll be sure to say goodbye before we go to the airport," Hunter announces as he pulls Devin out of the booth and walks him to the door.

Once outside, they get into the car, Hunter in the driver's seat, Devin on the passenger side, but they don't start the engine. Hunter rubs circles onto Devin's back while he concentrates on breathing. It's not a true panic attack or anything like that, but it's disconcerting. After a while Hunter asks, "You want to talk about it?"

Devin doesn't know where to start, but he can't keep this inside. "It just hit me that we're doing this. And it's all so amazing and what if you wake up tomorrow and don't want me anymore? Or what if you go up in your plane one day and don't come back? Before, it was just a crush I could shove to the side. Now it's my heart that you've got and I'm just—it's a little scary."

Hunter laughs, but not meanly. "Tell me about it. Why do you think I tried to run away from this, from you and what I feel?" He doesn't stop rubbing Devin's back. "But you said it yourself—we're partners. At work, sure. But in this, too. We're in it together. We're going to get scared; we're going to mess up sometimes. But we're going to figure it out together."

He's comforted by Hunter's words and by the complete certainty with which he says them. "Together. Okay."

"And if things get to be too much, you can always say duct tape." Hunter smiles.

"You want us to be able to safe word out of our relationship?"

"Not exactly, but we can still use it for those times when we need a little extra help."

"Okay." Devin looks at his—boyfriend?—and something else occurs to him. "So when we get back to SkyTrip, what are we going to tell the crew?"

"About us?"

"Yeah."

"We can tell them whatever you're comfortable telling them. We don't have to tell them anything at all."

"I think they might catch on when we're making out in the break room."

Hunter waggles his eyebrows. "You have plans to make out with me in the break room?"

"Hunter, we've been together for fifteen hours and we've already had sex like five times. You couldn't keep your hands to yourself in front of your ex-in-laws! I suppose we are in a bit of a honeymoon period, but are you honestly telling me you aren't going to be sexually harassing me at work?"

"I wouldn't if you didn't want me to," Hunter says.

Devin can see that he's completely serious. "Wow, well, I think I'll be okay with it. As long as we're not scandalizing our employees."

"Yes, professionalism must be maintained," Hunter says, but then he kisses Devin with tongue which detracts a bit from his statement. When they come up for air,

Hunter goes on, "Speaking of honeymoon periods, I think we should plan our next vacation."

"Already? We haven't even gotten back from the first one."

"Aren't you always telling me it's good to take breaks? I want to take one, with you, someplace warm where we can be mostly naked most of the time."

"I have no objections to that," Devin says, imagining a beach and a hotel room and Hunter's naked body. Nope. No objections.

"Great. You're way better at planning this stuff than me. You tell me when and where and I will show up for our sex vacation."

"Oh, it's a sex vacation now, is it?" God, could he love this man any more?

"Of course. Unless you want to make it an official honeymoon. But I don't want to rush you into anything."

"Honeymoon?" Devin squeaks out the word. Hunter seems perfectly calm talking about the possibility of them getting married, but then, he's Hunter. "Give me a few..." he considers what amount of time would be appropriate, considering they're less than a day into their relationship. Year? Months? "...weeks, at least."

Hunter grins. "You got it, babe."

TWENTY-FOUR

IT'S LATE when they finally get back home to Joshua Tree—nearly midnight, and it feels later, given how quickly they'd adjusted to East Coast time. The streets in town are quiet and empty. Hunter rolls down his window, lets the desert night air wash away the staleness of travel. The wind is dry and cool and sweet and reminds him more than anything else that he loves his adopted home. Going back to his hometown had been nice in a way, but he doesn't miss living there.

He tips his face toward the window; the air stirs his hair. He smiles.

Devin lets out a laugh from the driver's seat. "You look like a Labrador," he says, the fondness in his voice unmistakable.

He turns onto the road that leads to the little trailer park on the outskirts of the city limits. They'll be at Hunter's place in a few minutes. As glad as Hunter is to be home, he doesn't exactly know how to do this. He and Devin will see each other in a few hours at work. They can be apart for a night. No big deal. Just because they've been living in each other's pockets for days and Hunter's been able to reach out and touch him whenever he wants for last however many hours. Hunter's not so codependent that he can't cope without Devin.

The car rolls to a stop in front of Hunter's trailer. His truck is still there, still needs work. His motorcycle is safely under the cover where he left it. The place looks— well, it's been perfectly adequate for Hunter's needs since he moved here and all he required was a place to sleep between building up SkyTrip. But still, there's something...lonely about it.

"Well, here we are." Devin doesn't sound particularly excited about reaching their destination. "You'll be all right?"

"Sure. Yeah. I'll—I'll be fine. I'll see you tomorrow."

"Right. Of course. Or—"

Hunter seizes on the word. "Or?"

"Or, well—you know I've got a better coffee maker than you, and well, we could carpool to work. For the environment."

"Are you asking me to come home with you?"

"It's just that you probably don't have a drop of fresh milk and I've got the market at the end of my block and—"

Hunter stops Devin's adorably flustered words by putting a hand on his knee and leaning in to kiss them out of his mouth. Eventually, he stops kissing him long enough to say, "Yes, I'll come home with you. I already have my toothbrush and everything."

"True." Devin kisses him back and they get carried

away with that for a minute before Hunter realizes they should have waited until they got to Devin's apartment because after keeping his hands to himself on the plane and the airport and the drive, he needs Devin, like, immediately.

"Let's go," he says, pressing one last hard kiss to Devin's sexy mouth. "And I wouldn't mind if you stepped on it."

In answer, Devin peels away from the curb with a screech. He uncharacteristically breaks a couple of road rules on the way there.

Devin's apartment is on the second floor of a small complex that contains a pool and a gym for the residents to use. Hunter is chagrined to realize he's never been here before. He follows Devin up narrow stairs to a landing, and Devin uses his keys to open a door marked 4. The air inside is a little stale, but the place is clean and tidy, not surprisingly. And it's bigger than Hunter would have expected, a large living room attached to the open kitchen; a balcony off the living room overlooks the pool.

"You can put your stuff back here," Devin says, heading for the hallway. Hunter passes a bathroom door, then what appears to be an office, and follows Devin through the last door, which leads to a bedroom and another bathroom. Devin's room is tidy and simple, a queen-sized bed taking up most of the space. He's got an Andy Warhol-style lithograph of Debbie Harry from Blondie over his bed.

"Nice digs, babe," Hunter says. It's intimidating to realize that Devin, who's younger than him, has his shit together way better than Hunter ever has. Devin's an actual adult. And Hunter's in love with him. Which means he's going to have to step up his game. He thinks he's up to the challenge.

"Thanks. Yeah. There's plenty of room. I wasn't really looking for a two bedroom but this was the only one available at the time, and I thought maybe my parents would come visit, or my sister, but they're lazy bums, so my guest room has gone pretty much unused and, come to think of it, if you're serious about the whole, um, commitment thing, you should think about maybe just, um, well, it's too soon. But it would save on over-head, and you know I'm all about fiscal responsibility and—"

Hunter puts a finger over Devin's mouth. "Devin. I practically proposed to you earlier today. I'm not going to freak out at the idea of us living together. And I'm sure I'm going to love it. But you need to know that you have options. You might not like living with me, you know."

"Oh, I don't know about that." Devin smiles and wraps Hunter in a hug. "I already know you don't snore."

"But I come with a rusty truck and a noisy motorcy-cle, and I can't make coffee to save my life."

"I've got an extra parking space for the truck, I love motorcycles, so I can't wait for you take me for a ride on yours, and as for the coffee—well, I already make coffee for both of us."

"There you go, saving my life again."

"Anytime, Hunter darling. Anytime."

THEY DO carpool to work the following morning, and they're not even late. Louis is the first one they encounter. He's pulling into the parking lot in his Range Rover and lifts an eyebrow when they emerge from Devin's compact in unison.

"Your truck on the fritz again?" he asks.

Devin glances at Hunter. They'd sort of talked about how they were going to approach the whole telling people thing, but he wants to leave it to Hunter to set the tone, since it's his signature on the paychecks.

"Well, actually, it is," Hunter says as he walks around the car to Devin's side. "But we thought it made more sense to carpool since we were both coming from his place. Oh yeah, we're together now." Then he grabs Devin's hand and grins.

Devin's cheeks are burning as he turns to see how Louis is taking that in. The older man looks almost as if he's going to laugh at Hunter's joke, but then the reflexive smile fades and a different one, a genuine one, takes its place.

"Are you now?" Louis walks up and claps them both on the shoulder. His strong hand squeezes Devin's bicep in earnest congratulations. "Must have been an open bar at the wedding reception, huh?"

Devin laughs at how close Louis's guess hits. They could explain the whole part of the story where Hunter had asked Devin to pose as his boyfriend, but he doesn't think Louis would believe them. Who would honestly believe such a wild story anyway?

The three of them walk into the SkyTrip offices together, Louis pumping Hunter's free hand, and filling them in on a little of what they missed over their long weekend's absence.

"You're back!" Isabelle meets them in the hall. "What's going on? Why does Louis look like the cat who swallowed the canary?"

"Because I know something you don't. Can I tell her? Please let me tell her," Louis begs like one of his teenage daughters when they want the car keys.

"Er, go ahead," Devin answers. He should have known they'd lose control of the narrative— SkyTrip employees are a dedicated crew, but they're nosy bastards and terrible gossips, to boot.

"Hunter and Devin are together," he says as proudly as if he'd set them up himself.

Her face breaks into an uncharacteristically huge grin. "Splendid! I have to text Arianna about this, she's going to be so excited."

That gives Devin pause. Isabelle's oddly enthusiastic response notwithstanding, why would her high school French teacher wife be excited that he and Hunter are dating? He doesn't have time to think about it too much, because they're in the break room now, and Hunter's still holding his hand.

Will and Laney are chatting over coffee, and almost in unison the two of them snap their gazes to where Hunter and Devin's hands are joined, then Louis is doing the announcement thing while Isabelle taps away at her phone.

"Congrats, guys, seriously," Will says.

Laney's more caustic. "About damn time," she says, but she's smiling, and pulls them both into a hug.

"Wait, what do you mean?" Hunter asks, taking the words out of Devin's mouth.

Laney and Will exchange a look. "Well, you know, we just always figured you two would make a good couple," she says.

"Yeah, who else actually enjoys putting up with Hunter's nonsense?" Louis asks, rhetorically, Devin assumes.

"And Hunter never smiles as much as he does when he's with you, Devin," Isabelle says, looking up from her phone. "Arianna's delighted by the way. She wants to have you two over for dinner this weekend. Or we could go out—a double date."

"Oh. Wow." Devin's truly happy that his friends and coworkers are on board with this development, but he's slightly mortified, as well. Could they all see his crush on Hunter, plain as day?

"Sounds great," Hunter says. "But there's no rush. This is pretty new and besides, we're going to be busy moving this weekend."

"Moving?" Will asks.

"Er, Hunter's moving to my place. It's a shorter commute," he adds weakly.

"Oh, yeah, I can see you are both really worried about moving too quickly," Isabelle says dryly. "Well, fine. I'll take a raincheck, boys."

"In the meantime, I'm sure we all have plenty of work to do," Hunter says, trying to be stern and failing miserably.

"That's right, get to work you slackers," Devin echoes.

There's some grumbling, but they really do have customers later in the day to prepare for, so the crowd disperses. Once the break room is empty, Hunter pulls Devin in close, tucking his hands into the back pockets of his jeans. Devin relishes the feel of Hunter's hard, warm body against his, and the glint in his beautiful green eyes.

"That went shockingly well," Hunter says. "I thought we'd be surprising everyone, but it turns out they could see something we couldn't."

"Who knew that lot was so perceptive?" Devin agrees. "But now they're gone, it would be a shame to put this privacy to waste."

"Oh, yes, it would be terribly irresponsible to waste this opportunity," Hunter says, and then he kisses Devin senseless in the break room.

EPILOGUE

THEY'VE BEEN LIVING TOGETHER for three months—the happiest three months of Hunter's life—when Devin turns to him over coffee and breakfast on the balcony of their apartment and says, "I think I'm ready for that sex vacation, now. If you are."

Since coming back from Jillian's wedding, they've been extra busy at work. They even had to hire another instructor to keep up with demand. Hunter had almost forgotten about their plan to get away to someplace warm with lots of opportunities for naked Devin time. He's made the most of sharing a bed and an apartment with his boyfriend—they've made love in most of the obvious spots (couch, shower) and some less obvious ones (Devin's home office closet on one memorable occasion). Devin's been surprisingly open minded about having sex at SkyTrip, too, but only after hours, when it's just them. They can't seem to keep their hands off each other when alone in the hangar, or the office, the break room, and the —okay, so they don't technically need a sex vacation to have sex. But then Hunter realizes what Devin's really saying.

"Wait, sex vacation, as in... honeymoon?" He's been trying to be patient, hasn't wanted to push, since things are so good between them. There's really no need to take things to a different level. Except for the fact that Hunter wants to know that Devin's in this for the rest of their lives. He wants Devin's ring on his finger and his on Devin's. He wants the world to know how stupidly, utterly in love he is.

Devin smiles a secret little smile. "There's no ring at the bottom of your cup, but I've been waiting months to say this: Hunter, you're dearer to me than French roast, you're more addictive than cold brew, you're sweeter than a mochachino. Will you drink my coffee forever? Will you be my husband?"

It's all Hunter can do to hold himself back from getting Devin in a car and driving across the state line to Nevada to get married right there and then.

Instead, he jumps up from the table, heedlessly knocking some of their breakfast dishes to the ground in the process and pulls Devin as far as the living room floor. "Yes," he whispers. Then he shows him exactly how enthusiastic he is about becoming Mr. Hunter Pike-Smith. Twice.

A FEW WEEKS LATER, they have a small ceremony in the park officiated by Isabelle, who somewhere in her past was apparently certified to perform marriages, with the entire SkyTrip staff present. Devin's mum and dad and sister have turned up for once and have welcomed Hunter like another son. Jillian and Aaron have managed to get away from the hospital for the occasion, and Myrna and Gary are on hand, proud and tearful.

Hunter looks gorgeous in the dark gray suit Devin helped him pick out. Devin had protested that they could get married in jeans and he'd be fine with it, but Hunter had insisted. "Jillian and I didn't have a real wedding—we did the jeans and scrubs elopement thing and it kind of set the tone for the whole endeavor. She and I were a moment in time. You and I are forever, Devin. Besides, you look hot as fuck in a suit." Well, how could he say no to that?

The ceremony is simple and to the point, but there's not a dry eye in the house by the time Hunter and Devin exchange their vows, including the two grooms. Devin swipes furtively at his eyes after Hunter slips the plain gold band onto his finger, but Hunter's eyes are streaming with tears, and he doesn't even seem to care. When Isabelle gets to the bit where they finally get to kiss, Hunter tastes salty; Devin's going to associate that flavor with being deliriously happy for the rest of his life.

The reception is low-key—beer in coolers and Louis manning the grill. Devin loosens his tie and accepts Jillian's hug. She squeezes hard enough to break a rib, but in a nice way. "I'm so, so happy for you two," she whispers in his ear. He thinks he can hear a bit of a catch in her voice. He knows she means it, but that doesn't mean it's not a little hard, for all of them. Jillian was Hunter's first love. Devin's always going to feel slightly jealous of the connection she and Hunter have, but all the same, he's so grateful for Jillian. She saved Hunter's life once, kept him alive long enough for Devin to come into his life, and for that he'll always be thankful. Not to mention the whole wedding-date-debacle-turned-happily-ever-after. She couldn't have predicted how her second wedding could lead to this moment, but Devin couldn't be happier that it did.

Later, when everyone's sleepy and maybe a little drunk and all the lovely wedding clothes have become barbecue scented and Will's questionable DJ skills have resulted in far too much disco, Devin taps his husband on the shoulder, interrupting his conversation with Carlos, Laney's date. He's tired and horny and so in love with this man that it hurts.

"Hunter." He taps again, as Carlos keeps talking about the time he went bungee jumping in Switzerland. Hunter turns to him, eyebrows lifted. "Hunter, darling. Um. Do you know where the duct tape is?"

"The duct tape?" Hunter repeats with concern.

"Yeah. The duct tape. I need some. Right now."

"Oh, right." Hunter waves at Carlos, grabs Devin by the hand. "We've gotta go—"

"Get some duct tape?" Carlos sounds really confused.

"Exactly."

Without another thought for their guests Hunter and Devin make a break for it. They head for the parking lot, where Hunter's motorcycle is parked and has been adorned with streamers, tin cans, and a Just Married sign by some mischievous SkyTrip employee no doubt.

Hunter laughs and tosses Devin his helmet. They stop to kiss each other again, don their helmets, then climb onto the bike, Devin holding onto Hunter's waist tight. "Ready to go home, husband?" Hunter asks over the roar of the engine.

"I'm ready to go anywhere with you, husband," Devin answers.

Hunter revs the engine and pulls out of the parking lot. The cans clank and clatter behind them, and a passing car toots its horn in celebration. "Hold onto me, babe."

Devin's never planning to let go.

Thanks for reading! For more feel-good, small-town m/m romance, subscribe to my newsletter at
ellewatersbooks.substack.com
and get a free story.

xoxo, Elle

ABOUT THE AUTHOR

Fueled by chocolate and canned wine, Elle Waters writes steamy, feel-good, small town romances with guaranteed happy endings. She lives with her family in Connecticut. Sign up for her newsletter at ellewatersauthor.com to hear about her next release!

Elle loves to hear from readers at elle@ ellewatersauthor.com.

facebook.com/ElleWatersAuthor

instagram.com/ellewatersbooks

amazon.com/~/e/B091FZQ4PZ

bookbub.com/authors/elle-waters

reamstories.com/ellewaters

www.ingramcontent.com/pod-product-compliance
Lightning Source LLC
Chambersburg PA
CBHW031603310726
48974CB00003B/789